THE RYZHKOV VENDETTA

A Mark Ericksen Thriller Book 2

BARRY L. BECKER

D0057345

"The supreme art of war is to subdue the enemy without fighting."
Sun Tzu, author of The Art of War

Chapter One

On March 21, 2011, Anthony "Tony" Ferrari was seated in the Four Seasons Hotel George V's Le Cinq Restaurant. He just finished his breakfast of café au lait and a croissant, Norwegian smoked salmon, baguette, jams, and orange juice. He spotted the waiter and motioned for his check. He then heard his secure cell phone ringing. On the third ring he checked the caller ID, and noticed the call was from a German cell phone number. He picked it up and said, "I'll call you back in five minutes."

A few minutes later, the waiter handed him the bill.

"Thank you," Ferrari said. He placed thirty-five dollars on the table, picked up his briefcase and suitcase, and walked toward the lobby.

Ferrari stood about six feet tall and maintained a lean, athletic build. The fifty-two-year-old looked distinguished with his wavy dark brown hair, inquisitive dark brown eyes, a Roman nose, and strands of gray by his temples. He fit in at the luxurious and opulent hotel, where celebrities, diplomats, business executives, royalty, and politicians stayed. He wore a brown leather calfskin Italian sports jacket, a designer blue-and-gold dress shirt open at the collar, and navy-blue casual slacks, and completing his suave, dignified appearance were expensive brown leather Testoni shoes.

He noticed an empty chair in the lobby. After sitting down and placing his luggage to the side, he picked up his cell phone and called the number back.

"Gerhard Richter speaking," the voice said in German.

"Wolfgang here," Ferrari said.

"All right. When you arrive at St. Pancras Station this afternoon, tell the taxi driver to go to the Starbucks on Pancras. Tell him to wait a few minutes. Go inside and look for my brother Egon. He is expecting you. He is in his thirties, wearing a blue Columbia sports jacket and a Chelsea FC cap. Egon will be sitting down, and once he spots you, his right hand will be raised. He will give you my birthday gift and my cell phone number. When you arrive at the hotel, please call that number."

Ferrari had already met Gerhard in Monte Carlo six months earlier and they had agreed to using these names.

"Affirmative," Ferrari said in German. He figured Russian intelligence had accumulated hundreds of pictures of him while he was stationed at the US Embassy in Moscow and, more recently, when he was chief-of-station at the US Embassy in Bern.

Ferrari thought, *Egon should easily recognize me.*

Ferrari had spent the last seven days working with his client at their Berlin and Paris headquarters on security issues. Tomorrow he would finish up with his client's London headquarters located in the Mayfair district. Ferrari checked out of the hotel. The bellman waved the first taxi in line to move up the hotel driveway.

Wearing dark sunglasses and carrying his suitcase and briefcase, he arrived at the Gare du Nord train station. He glanced at his Omega dive watch and noted the time: 10:45 am. It was a habit of his to check his watch when waiting in lines.

He stood in line for several minutes before passing through security and customs. He proceeded to a waiting area. He put down his suitcase and briefcase and made a call on his encrypted cell phone to a secure landline phone number at the US Embassy in London.

"Hello, Bob, it's Mario Ivanelli," he said, using his old alias.

"Hello, Mario. When you arrive, please call my cell phone number."

"Affirmative," said Ferrari.

He boarded the Eurostar and found his way to the Standard Premier section. The train departed at 11:13 am. It would arrive in London at 12:39 pm. He glanced around the full compartment and noticed a couple in their early forties with their two children sitting across the aisle from him. They looked happy and wore expensive clothes. He thought about his ex-wife and his two kids, a fifteen-year-old son and his twenty-four-year-old daughter who taught kindergarten. Three years ago, when he and his wife divorced, it had been hardest on his young son. Over the years, being away from his family had created lots of stress in their marriage, in addition to the danger he faced in his line of work.

Over the past three years, selling their two-thousand-square-foot house on Douglass Avenue in upper-middle-class Falls Church, Virginia, the divorce costs, the damage caused by the 2008 wall street financial meltdown on their two rental properties, splitting the assets, the alimony, and now paying off college loans created a financial burden. Seven months ago, his eighty-year-old father had an accident rendering him paralyzed from the waist down. Both he and his brother shared the eight-thousand-dollar monthly expenses for his father's nursing home in Florida. His brother lived close to their father and took an active role in assisting him.

Ferrari's thoughts were interrupted as the Eurostar sped through the Chunnel, separating France from England. He marveled at the Eurostar train's speed, which reached 180 miles an hour in spots. The distance from Paris to London via Chunnel was approximately 214 miles.

LONDON

Upon arriving at St. Pancras Station at 12:40 pm, Ferrari carried his suitcase and briefcase to an awaiting taxi. He asked the driver to take him to Starbucks on Pancras. He arrived ten minutes later and noticed

Egon sitting down. They had a brief conversation, and Egon gave him a birthday gift.

He left Starbucks and jumped back into the taxi. Ferrari removed his sunglasses as he entered St. Ermin's Hotel on Caxton Street by St. James Park. Registering for his room, he produced his passport and chatted with the front desk clerk. The hotel had the distinction of being used during World War II as the headquarters of the British Intelligence Services.

Since it was too early for check-in, he handed his luggage and briefcase to the bell captain to place in security. He took the two tags from the bell captain and walked over to the lobby sofas to sit down. After opening the gift box, Ferrari spent a few minutes familiarizing himself with the burner cell phone inside. He walked outside the hotel and called Gerhard's cell phone number from the burner.

"Hello Gerhard, it's Wolfgang," Ferrari said.

"Wolfgang, take a taxi to the London Eye. Look for a man wearing a Chelsea football club cap and carrying a Nikon camera with a telescopic lens. I'll be in line around 3:00 pm."

"Check out my mustache and Chelsea football cap. See you soon."

He thought for a moment. Sweat ran down his forehead. Why am I doing this, he asked himself. If I change my mind, what can they do to me? What if I offer to pay them back? He then made a call to his friend Bob's direct encrypted Virginia cell phone number. The man at the US Embassy in London picked up the phone. "Bob speaking."

"Mario here."

"When did you arrive? "A few hours ago."

"Mario, please hold a few seconds while I take this call."

"No problem."

A minute later, he pressed his cell phone again. "When I picked up the call, I didn't recognize this cell phone number. Is it a burner phone?"

"Yes, it is."

"Okay, is seven a good time for dinner?" he asked.

"Yes. Where?"

"Let's meet at the Grill at the Dorchester Hotel."

"Okay," said Ferrari, and hung up.

He walked up to the bellmen at the front entrance of the hotel. "Please get me a taxi."

"Yes, sir."

Ferrari arrived at a McDonald's and went right into the men's restroom. He placed a thick mustache above his upper lip, a Chelsea football club cap on his head, made final adjustments, and left the restaurant. Ferrari walked several blocks before approaching the London Eye ferris wheel. His brow was wet with sweat. He realized his meeting with Gerhard was crossing the red line. From this day forward, his life could be in danger. After surveying the area where hundreds of people lined up, Ferrari finally saw a man with the Chelsea football cap on his head. In his early forties, the Slavic-looking man had blondish-brown hair, a long thin nose, high cheek-bones, and cold blue-gray eyes. He was about 6'2" and powerfully built like a gymnast.

Ferrari walked up to the man, smiled, and said in German, "Good to see you again."

The man smiled back. They waited in line for about ten minutes before entering the London Eye capsule, which overlooked the Thames River. Ferrari and Gerhard moved to the farthest point facing the bridge and the Parliament building. Five minutes into the ride, he handed Gerhard a small tin box of breath mints. Gerhard placed the box in his inside jacket pocket.

"In the mint box is a USB drive with all the details, names, addresses, etc. It is encrypted in the agreed-upon software the boss recommended. Please remember the name EyeD4 Systems in Wilsonville, Oregon, and their key employees, Mark Ericksen and Lars Wahlberg," Ferrari said.

Gerhard shook his head, smiled, and whispered into his ear, "In three days, your money will be in your bank account."

"Thank you."

When the ride was over, each man went their separate ways.

Ferrari entered a hotel near the Parliament building, darted to the men's room, opened a stall door, removed his mustache, and threw it into the trash. After exiting the hotel, he walked toward the Parliament building and hailed a taxi to his hotel. Having spent nine years as a United States military intelligence officer and the last twenty-one with the Central Intelligence Agency, he knew his knowledge and expertise would be an asset to the American defense community. His retirement from the Agency was official on November 15, 2010.

On January 15, 2011, his firm, *AUF Consulting Group*, focused on international risk and business intelligence consulting. A prestigious Washington DC law firm retained his consulting company to handle its aerospace and defense corporation clients. The aerospace corporation's worldwide headquarters resided in Reston, Virginia.

At seven in the evening, Ferrari spotted Richmond, walked toward him, shook hands, and went to the Grill. Richmond's four-person security detail followed the men. Richmond was an African American, about fifty-years-old, approximately 5'10" with a muscular build, and dressed in a three-piece dark blue pin-striped suit. He had large brown eyes and a neat trim mustache. He spent twelve years in the US Army as a member of the 5th Special Forces unit. When he left the service as a major, he was recruited by the CIA in 1996.

Richmond was the CIA chief-of-station in London, and his name was an alias. They followed the host to a table covered in white linens. The host provided them with the Grill's menu for the evening. He looked forward to meeting his old friend. The last thing Ferrari did not want to discuss was his domestic violence charges cited in the 2008 divorce.

"How's retirement, Tony?"

"I'm a business intelligence consultant on retainer with a Washington DC law firm. My first project is with one of their major defense contractors *Engstrom-Knight Aerospace*."

"I'll bet the money is better than what we get paid."

"I'm happy with the consulting fees," Ferrari said, smiling.

"Where are you living these days?" Richmond asked.

"I bought a condo in Alexandria on Madison Street. It's a two bedroom two bath unit, with a pool, a gym, and a view."

"Glad to hear you're doing well," said Richmond.

They had met years ago at the CIA during their German language training in the States. In 1997, Richmond moved to the US Embassy in Berlin as a political attache', while Ferrari went off to the US Embassy in Vienna in the same capacity. During the period from 2004-2006, the men worked at CIA Headquarters in Langley, Virginia. It was during this time both men and their wives socialized and were good friends. They both enjoyed talking about their military experience during *Operation Desert Storm*. In 2007-2008, Ferrari became the political attache' at the US Embassy in Moscow, Russia. He spent eight months back at CIA headquarters in 2008, and his last two years, 2009-2010, as CIA chief of station at the US Embassy in Bern, Switzerland.

The waiter approached their table with two glasses of water and asked, "What would you gentlemen like to start with?"

"I would like to order the Dover sole with the seasonal vegetables and a bowl of blue lobster chowder soup," said Richmond.

"I'll also go with the blue lobster chowder soup, the Black Angus beef fillet, and your potatoes and seasonal vegetables," said Ferrari.

The waiter asked him, "How would you like your Black Angus cooked?"

"Medium, please."

"Have you had a chance to look at the wine list?" asked the waiter.

Richmond answered, "Just pick a nice Cabarnet Sauvignon from Napa."

"We have several exquisite Cabarnets from that area," the waiter replied. "They start at ninety-five British pounds and go up."

"Please get us one in that price range."

"I'll have it brought to your table shortly," replied the waiter.

"Bob, when are you planning on retiring?" Ferrari asked.

"My wife is pushing me to retire next year, but I would like to stay with the Agency for a few more years."

"Then what would you like to do after you retire?"

"Not sure. More than likely work for a lobbyist on K Street or a defense contractor."

He told Ferrari his real name a few years ago. Ken Washington and

Tony Ferrari worked in the shadow world, and their real names while in the employ of the CIA were classified as top-secret. Ferrari hoped Richmond would volunteer if he had heard rumors of another mole in the CIA but decided not to ask him. Over the past thirty years, the CIA had discovered three moles within its ranks: Howard E. Lee, Aldrich Ames, and Jim Nicholson. During that time, the FBI uncovered a mole within its own ranks: Robert Hanssen. Those convicted Russian spies did devastating damage to the United States of America. MI6 had moles like Kim Philby, and the KGB had Oleg Gordievsky, who spied for Britain's MI6 and did the most damage to Russia.

Ferrari looked at him and said, "Have you heard anything from your sources about Igor Kublanov's life being in danger?"

Richmond looked up with surprise and shrugged. "No, I haven't heard anything from our Russian assets."

"I heard he is secretly supporting the opposition in next year's presidential elections," said Ferrari.

"If he wants to continue owning an energy company and enjoying his billions, he shouldn't underestimate Prime Minister Mikhail Gorshkov," said Richmond.

Ferrari nodded his head, "Gorshkov will have no trouble winning the presidential election. He is definitely in total control."

"I agree."

After enjoying the meal, wine, and good conversation, two hours passed. The CIA station chief paid for the dinner. They left the restaurant with the security detail in tow. They got into the limo and drove to Ferrari's hotel and dropped him off.

Ferrari expected the Russian Foreign Intelligence Service (SVR), had a case officer or two following them. He would not be surprised to find the British Domestic Secret Intelligence Service (MI5) case officers following the Russians. He knew the games spies play.

Chapter Two

On March 23, 2011, Poul Kastrup, CEO and founder of *Cyberburst Communications*, was surrounded by the Executive Vice-President/COO, Logan Mitchell, and his CFO, Albert Alioto. They were seated around a large redwood table at their headquarters on Page Mill Road in Palo Alto.

Kastrup founded the company in 1995, after a successful marketing management career in the aerospace and defense industry. His last position was as vice-president of Raytheon.

"I know you're extremely high on Mark Ericksen for this position," Mitchell said to Kastrup, "but do you believe he is the right candidate?" asked Mitchell.

"Your candidate at *A7 Aerospace Systems*, is excellent, but Ericksen is well-connected within the Department of Defense and the intelligence community."

Kastrup had the look of a Marine drill sergeant, a full head of wavy silver-gray hair, a jutting-jaw, and hairy eyebrows with piercing, sparkling light blue eyes. He was of average height and weight, with a lean and athletic build, high cheekbones, and a trim beard.

Staring down at both men, and with an authoritative voice, Kastrup said, "Ericksen not only served with distinction as a Navy

SEAL Team Six officer but for the past nine years he has worked for three defense contractors delivering impressive results. He joined *EyeD4 Systems* in 2006 as their senior vice-president of marketing and sales, and their sales significantly increased When we acquired the company in November 2009, we promoted him to president and CEO. The company's sales went from $7 million in 2009 and will reach about $50 million dollars by the end of this September. That is proven leadership!" Kastrup abruptly looked at his executive team and continued, "I've made my decision, and that's final, gentlemen!"

Mitchell looked grim. "Poul, we're going to support your decision." The next day, Mark Ericksen woke up at 6:00 am, put on his jogging suit, sneakers, and Oregon State University baseball cap and went out the door of his hotel room. The handsome Danish-born, sandy gold-haired, blue-eyed muscular-built forty-year-old was an inch over six feet, with high cheekbones, and a Hollywood movie actor's looks. He left the Rosewood Sand Hill Hotel on Sand Hill Road and ran at a good clip until he reached the Stanford Shopping Center. He stopped, wiped his face with his handkerchief, and began the jog back up the hill. After going to his room, he took a cold shower, put on a sharp dress suit, a white shirt, and a blue tie.

Kastrup, Mitchell, and Alioto were seated around the conference table in the CEO's office. The time was 8:30 am and the intercom buzzed.

"Mr. Kastrup, Mr. Ericksen has arrived in the headquarters' lobby," the executive assistant said.

"Please have the security officer issue him a badge and escort him to the fifth floor."

"Yes, sir."

The Department of Defense had granted Cyberburst Communications a facility clearance, enabling top-secret security clearances for several departments within its headquarters and several manufacturing plants and divisions.

When the elevator arrived on the fifth floor, Ericksen walked twenty feet to the executive office door. A receptionist saw him through the video camera outside the secure lobby office. She pressed a button that opened the door to the executive office. She called Kastrup's staff assistant to meet her in the executive office. The staff assistant opened the thick oak door and entered and closed the door. She met Ericksen and turned to face the iris biometrics system, which was on the wall next to the door.

The staff assistant looked into the unit, and the system recognized her iris in real-time and, within a few seconds, matched her template stored in the CPU of the biometrics system, activating a door shunt that opened the oak door to the top-secret offices. The staff assistant provided the time of entry.

Ericksen walked with an air of confidence into Kastrup's spacious wood-paneled executive office. After making eye contact with both Mitchell and the chief financial officer, Ericksen shook hands with everyone. He sat opposite Kastrup and looked directly at him.

"Mark, we would like to offer you the position of vice-president of strategic planning and business development," Kastrup said. "This position's primary responsibility is analyzing and evaluating emerging biometrics and satellite espionage technology companies. We're interested in these fields for potential acquisitions."

Ericksen gently nodded his head. Then Alioto gave Kastrup the compensation package to review.

Kastrup continued, "The starting salary is $300,000 plus fifteen thousand shares of *Cyberburst Communications*. You already own ten thousand shares from *EyeD4 Systems*. If you accept our offer, you need to start on August 1. Would you be interested in joining our company?"

Ericksen broke into a big smile. "I am grateful for this opportunity and gladly accept your generous offer."

The other men stood to offer congratulations. "Welcome aboard," Mitchell said.

"Congratulations," Alioto said.

Everyone left the office except Ericksen and Kastrup. Displayed on the wall were Kastrup's college diplomas, a B.S. degree from the University of California, Berkeley, and an MBA from Stanford

University. Photos of his wife, two adult children, and grandchildren were on a redwood credenza table.

"We're looking forward to attending your upcoming wedding in May."

Ericksen smiled, "You'll have a wonderful time."

Four hours later, Ericksen boarded a flight to Portland on Alaska Airlines from San Jose International Airport. He had a remarkable history over the past decade. If it were not for his last operation in Afghanistan, he probably would still be in the Navy and might have reached the rank of commander by this time.

In April 2002, he was second-in-command of an elite tier-one Bravo team consisting of eighteen operators of the Joint Special Operations Command, JSOC, departing out of Bagram Air Base, Afghanistan, on a high-level target operation. He was a navy lieutenant of *DEVGRU*, commonly known as Seal Team-Six, who was all about duty, honor, and country. His loyalty focused on the mission and his teammates.

During that operation, his commanding officer of Bravo team, Jeb Templeton, a Delta Force major, was wounded. Ericksen saved his life and took over the mission. Several men died on that operation, and the deputy commander of JSOC ordered him to kill his Afghan intelligence officer who was part of the team. The commander, a bird colonel, told him they received information from a Pashtun village elder who claimed the Afghan intel officer was a Taliban member. Ericksen worked with this intel officer and did not believe it, thus, killing him was the furthest thing from his mind.

The commander was furious with Ericksen, who ignored the kill order. Several minutes later, the colonel lied to him and said he received Agency intercepts confirming the allegations. Ericksen had no choice but to kill the Afghan intelligence officer.

The next day after Bravo team's briefing, he found out from Dex, the CIA operations chief at Bagram Air Base, they never had intercepts on the Afghan intel officer. Ericksen's JSOC deputy commander lied to him. He could not ask for an investigation into the commander's criminal malfeasance because the one witness to this travesty was involved in the conspiracy. From that day forward, his guilt and depression led to PTSD. To make matters worse, a year earlier, his wife died in an automobile accident.

In May 2002, he resigned his commission at the U.S. Naval Special Warfare Development headquarters at Dam Creek, Virginia. Ericksen was awarded the Silver Star in 2002 for bravery during *Operation Enduring Freedom* and received the Purple Heart from a classified mission in North Africa a year earlier. Over the next several years he worked for three defense contractors, maintaining his top-secret security clearance while concealing his PTSD.

Four years later, Templeton, who as deputy director for the Department of Defense's biometrics and forensics enterprise, recommended him for senior vice-president of marketing position at *EyeD4 Systems* in Wilsonville, Oregon.

In July 2009, the CEO of *EyeD4 Systems* sold the company to *Cyberburst Communications*, and Ericksen became the CEO in November. Now seventeen months after becoming the CEO of a subsidiary of the Palo Alto corporation, he accepted a senior management position at corporate headquarters.

WILSONVILLE, OREGON

Ericksen arrived at his office at 5:00 pm. He briefed his three top officers at *EyeD4 Systems* about accepting a senior marketing position at *Cyberburst Communications* in Palo Alto.

Sitting in that meeting were Jeb Templeton, his senior vice president of marketing, Lars Wahlberg, his COO, and Sofia Kastrup, the chief financial officer, and the daughter of Poul Kastrup.

One of the conditions Kastrup had stipulated for acquiring *EyeD4 Systems* from the privately held company's founder was that he had to hire his daughter Sofia Kastrup. Since Sofia Kastrup had an MBA from Harvard University and was a CPA with a Silicon Valley software company, its CEO and founder did not have any objections. A Portland law firm recruited his daughter's husband, and Poul Kastrup could not be happier for their move to Oregon.

They were excited about Ericksen's new position. He told them he would start on August 1 and recommended them for new positions within the company with *Cyberburst Communications'* top management's approval.

WEST LINN, OREGON

In October 2010, Kate McDonald, an attractive thirty-six-year-old redhead with sparkling green eyes, moved in with Ericksen and joined an executive recruiting firm in the banking and financial sector in Lake Oswego, Oregon. Shortly after that, they became engaged. She was happy about their upcoming wedding in May. McDonald's exciting life started when she left her home in Sandpoint, Idaho, to attend Stanford University. She was a member of Pi Beta Phi sorority.

The CIA approached McDonald after she graduated from Stanford University in 2000 with a degree in international relations and German language proficiency. After extensive vetting, they hired and trained her a year later into their directorate of operations. She assumed several aliases over her brief career at the CIA. Her first assignment was as a political counselor at the American Embassy in Berlin. In 2005-2007, under a pseudonym (*Elizabeth Caldwell*), she attended the International Institute for Management Development (IMD) in Switzerland and received an MBA in banking and finance. Proficient in both French and German, she landed a job with a Swiss firm in Geneva.

One year later, she became a manager at *Prentice and Aubert*, a New York executive recruiting firm and a shell company for the CIA. In that position, she recruited talented Swiss candidates for Swiss banking and financial firms from her Geneva-based location and worked as a NOC (a non-official CIA officer). Her intelligence mission was to turn over those new hires' names to *Dave Jacobson*, an alias

Lars Wahlberg used. He was a NOC assigned to work as an economics counselor at the U.S. Embassy in Bern. Once he received their names, his job was to turn them into assets.

In 2009, the Agency received actionable intelligence about the terrorist mastermind's mission to attack American cities. Ericksen and McDonald were part of *Operation Avenging Eagles,* a mission tasked by the CIA to sabotage a terrorist mastermind's plans aided by Russian arms dealers to attack two American cities with nuclear suitcase bombs. The mission's secondary objective focused on discovering money laundering operations in private Swiss numbered accounts linked to Russian arms dealers, terrorists, corrupt politicians, government, and military leaders.

There was not a week that went by where McDonald did not experience the terrible nightmares from her time being abducted in Switzerland. She never forgot the trauma she suffered from Sergei Ryzhkov and Oleg Kupchenko in Switzerland. Nor did she ever forget the torture and sexual assault the Russian arms dealer Kupchenko inflicted on her.

When McDonald left the CIA in late November 2009, she went back to her hometown in Idaho. Over the next several months, she received treatment for PTSD that lifted her spirits. When she moved in with Ericksen, he provided her love and additional support during her battle. She continued therapy with a Lake Oswego psychologist.

Ericksen arrived at their home around 7:00 pm. McDonald greeted him with hugs and kisses. They were heading up to Mount Hood tomorrow afternoon and planned to spend two days skiing at both Timberline Lodge ski area and Mt. Hood Meadows. During a nice dinner at the Portland Chart House they celebrated the exciting news of his new position with *Cyberburst Communications* in Palo Alto and their promising future.

Chapter Three

MOSCOW

On March 25, 2011, Gerhard flew from Berlin on Russian airline Aeroflot and arrived at Sheremetyevo International Airport Moscow at 4:30 pm. His bodyguards met him and escorted him into an armored Mercedes limo outside. He went to the Moscow International Business Center and walked directly to the Naberezhnaya Tower entrance, located at 10 Presnenskaya Nab, Block C, at 6:00 pm.

The sixty-five-story tower stood near the Moscow River, about two miles west of Red Square. Many well-known international corporations, major Russian banks, and industrial firms had their headquarters in the building. A contingent of FSB (Russian Domestic Intelligence Services) officers also had an office in the building.

Gerhard approached the elevator banks, went to the single elevator marked 50th floor, and pressed the button. When the elevator door opened, he looked directly at a camera mounted on the side wall. He looked into the camera and pressed a button. The facial recognition system immediately took a picture of his face and compared it to the template housed in the computer. Within five seconds, the match was successful, and the elevator door closed and lifted off.

Fifteen seconds later, the elevator arrived at *Ryzhkov Energy and*

Mining Company's headquarters offices on the fiftieth floor. The company occupied the entire floor consisting of ten office suites. He entered the executive lobby, and an administrative assistant immediately welcomed him.

"Viktor Vladimirovich Sorokin, welcome back," she said in Russian. "Mr. Ryzhkov is expecting you."

"Thank you."

Sorokin served as Mr. Alexander Ryzhkov's head of security and trusted advisor for the past three years. The former Spetsnaz captain and SVR intelligence operative used many aliases in his secret life, and Gerhard was his latest. He walked past several office suites before entering Ryzhkov's expansive office. At forty-one-years-old, he projected an air of confidence and strength as he strode forward.

When he entered the executive suite, Ryzhkov gave him a big hug and said in Russian, "Viktor Vladimirovich, I'm glad to see you."

Sorokin smiled, removed a thumb drive from his suit pocket, and gave it to Ryzhkov. "Good job. I presume everything went well with our asset?"

"Wolfgang came through for us." He reached into his suit pocket and handed Ryzhkov a three-page letter. "I decrypted the USB drive he gave me. It lists the operatives' names on *Operation Avenging Eagles*, addresses of both the company, and their home residences."

Ryzhkov picked up the intercom and spoke to one of his assistants, "Please bring us some tea."

"Yes, sir."

Ryzhkov was fifty-nine-years-old, medium height, with a full head of steely gray hair, and a muscular build. His face looked more like a prizefighter's, broken nose and eyebrows filled with scars. He had graduated from a Russian military academy and years later earned a master's degree in geology from Moscow State University. Ryzhkov acquired the company six years ago as a reward for his loyalty to Russia's current prime minister, his best boyhood friend. He cherished many happy memories from his Leningrad childhood. A year later, he changed the company's name, and since that time, accelerated the company's operations and growth. Last year's revenues reached $10 billion.

An hour later, Ryzhkov picked up his secure landline and called Prime Minister Mikhail Yuryevich Gorshkov.

Gorshkov's chief of staff Sokurov picked up the phone. "Hello General Ryzhkov, Prime Minister Gorshkov is not available at this time. Can I help you?"

"It is important for me to see him immediately. It is about our friend Wolfgang. What is the earliest time you can schedule me in?"

"Tuesday, the 29th at ten in the morning."

"That will work. Thank you."

BRITISH AIR FLIGHT: LONDON-WASHINGTON, D.C.

On March 27, two hours after take-off, Ferrari put on blinders and reflected. He thought about Ryzhkov. He had first met him when Ryzhkov served as the military attaché with general's rank in the Russian Embassy in Berlin. Ferrari served in the American Embassy from 1997-1998. They met at various foreign functions and enjoyed socializing. During 2007-2008, when he worked at the US Embassy in Moscow, he renewed his contact with Ryzhkov.

In August 2010, they met again at a United Nations function in Geneva. After a few drinks, Ryzhkov mentioned that he had something important to tell him, but that this was not the place to talk. He asked Ferrari if he could meet him in Monte Carlo in December. He had just resigned from the Agency and felt less pressure of being under surveillance. Ryzhkov discovered through Russian Intelligence in 2009 that Mario Ivanelli's real name was Anthony Ferrari.

Ferrari had reservations about meeting with a powerful Russian oligarch and a close friend of Prime Minister Gorshkov. However, he agreed, and a meeting was set up at the Hotel de Paris in Monte Carlo, Monaco, for Tuesday morning, December 7, 2010. He could not be sure if Ryzhkov was interested in spying for the Americans. How could a former general of the GRU, the Russian Military Intelligence Service's Main Intelligence Directorate, and a multi-billionaire energy

CEO become a traitor? Plus, when Ferrari factored in that Ryzhkov was a childhood friend of Russia's prime minister, it did not make any sense. Ferrari thought Ryzhkov must want something from him.

Ryzhkov hated the Americans just as much as his good friend Prime Minister Gorshkov. He had been a Lt. Colonel in Afghanistan in 1986 commanding a Spetsnaz battalion. The war endured from 1979-1989 and killed over fourteen thousand Russian soldiers. The Russians could not hold on to the Mujahideen's territory because the CIA provided the Afghan government with Stinger missiles, that destroyed many aircraft.

On December 6, Ferrari arrived in Monaco and met with several bank managers in Monte Carlo about opening a private numbered bank account.

On the 7th, they met in Ferrari's room. After spending several minutes exchanging pleasantries and drinking Stolichnaya vodka, Ryzhkov looked straight into Ferrari's eyes, and with a stern voice told him in English, "I need the names of those people who were on the CIA mission called *Operation Avenging Eagles.*"

Ferrari was in debt, but at that moment, he was interested to hear what the oligarch might offer him. However, he had to be extremely careful because the Russians were masters of blackmail, intimidation, and murder. He thought at that moment, the Agency never treated him with a faster career path, and it would not take long for the Russians to get this information eventually. Ferrari expected he would be assigned to the prestigious post of station chief in London in 2009, but CIA director Sullivan appointed Washington instead. He was tired of being in debt and now realized he was crossing a line that spelled traitor.

"General, it will cost you three hundred thousand dollars."

Ryzhkov did not want to haggle with Ferrari on this figure.

"Tony, I will give you one-hundred-thousand dollars as a down payment in cash right now and the balance of two-hundred-thousand to be wired to a private Monte Carlo bank of your choosing after I receive the information."

"Alexander, you got a deal," said Ferrari.

Ryzhkov opened his suitcase, took out one-hundred-thousand dollars and placed them into an expensive Italian leather case. "The money is in here," he said, as he pointed to the briefcase and handed it over to Ferrari.

Ryzhkov stood and knocked on the second bedroom to the suite.

His head of security appeared and surprised Ferrari.

"Let me introduce you to my chief-of-staff, Viktor Sorokin. He will be a key person who will work with you."

Ferrari reached out with his right hand and shook Sorokin's hand. "Glad to meet you."

"From this point on, I'll call you Wolfgang, and I'm Gerhard Richter," said Sorokin in German.

"Understood."

Ferrari turned to face Ryzhkov and reverted to English.

"I have made several inquiries, and the bank I will be using is Monch and Schneider Private Bank in Monte Carlo. After I deposit the money this afternoon, I'll provide you with my bank's private numbered account."

"I'll be in my room awaiting your call," said the oligarch. They shook hands and smiled.

Ferrari thought this would be a one-time effort on his part and worth the risk. He called Ryzhkov's Swiss encrypted cell phone 41-41-5536428 on his Virginia cell number. The oligarch maintained a second home in Zug as well as an office. After he answered the phone, Ferrari provided him with his private numbered account.

Chapter Four

MOSCOW

The state dacha in Novo-Ogaryovo was a palatial estate in the Odintsovsky District, west of the city of Moscow. Ryzhkov's armored Mercedes Benz limo stayed close behind the Mercedes driving his bodyguards. Behind his limo, a third Mercedes carried more bodyguards. The whole convoy pulled up to the prime minister's driveway.

Ryzhkov had retired six years ago as the commanding general of the GRU. He had a net worth of approximately $3 billion dollars and he wielded considerable influence in Russia's energy and mining industries.

Ryzhkov and Gorshkov grew up in Leningrad, lived two blocks from each other, were classmates in grammar school, and best friends. When Gorshkov's father was asked to join President Nikita Khrushchev's administration in 1963, the family moved to Moscow.

Ryzhkov served Prime Minister Gorshkov on critical operations, several of which dealt with killing traitors. However, the Russian strategic mission involving a Saudi terrorist mastermind, which had been uncovered and destroyed by the CIA, impacted Russian oil exports. In that operation, Ryzhkov's younger brother Sergei, his former staff advisor, Oleg Kupchenko, and many Russian Spetsnaz bodyguards had lost their lives in Switzerland and the Middle East.

Sergei Ryzhkov had been a former KGB and FSB intelligence colonel. Kupchenko was a retired Spetsnaz colonel, and an advisor to General Ryzhkov ten years ago at the GRU. He was also a senior member of the Russian organized crime syndicate in Moscow. Alexander Ryzhkov wanted revenge for the murder of his team and the destruction of the mission. The USB drive he now possessed revealed the identities of the principal operatives in the CIA operation that had led to those losses.

As he sat outside the prime minister's office awaiting Sokurov's prompt to enter, he thought about the failed mission. It began three years earlier when Gorshkov had given him approval to infiltrate a Saudi terrorist's internal organization. The overriding plan was to sell four Russian nuclear suitcase bombs, each containing three kilograms of fissionable plutonium and highly enriched uranium to the terrorist sleeper-cell network, along with the list of two US cities to target. The terrorist attacks would create another 9/11 and bolster American desire for revenge. The uproar from the American government would force a boycott of Saudi oil and encourage other allies to do the same. This action would create a significant imbalance of oil on the market and accelerate demand, benefiting Russia.

When Gorshkov graduated from Moscow State University with a law degree, the KGB recruited him and sent him to the Academy of Foreign Intelligence. After finishing his foreign intelligence training, he began his career at the KGB. Years later, his last KGB position was second-in-command as a lieutenant colonel at the Soviet Embassy in East Berlin. Both Gorshkov and Ryzhkov were devastated when the Soviet Union broke down. They hated the Americans for being the driving force in that effort.

Gorshkov's chief-of-staff entered the prime minister's office.

"Sir, General Alexander Leonidovich Ryzhkov is here for his appointment."

"Have him come in," Gorshkov calmly said.

As Ryzhkov entered, Gorshkov stood up, walked forward, and shook his hand. He wore a Patek Phillipe watch on his right wrist.

At six feet in height and 180 pounds, the lean and muscular Gorshkov excelled in handball. He had earned two championship titles from the Russian Handball Federation in Moscow in the late 80s. His brilliant mind had no time for small talk; he was all business and could turn into a cold-blooded killer in the blink of an eye, should he be challenged. He enjoyed playing handball with Ryzhkov, who also excelled in the sport. Gorshkov usually won.

Gorshkov had a full head of dark brown hair, streaked with gray, and piercing pale blue eyes.

"Sasha, my old friend," he said, as he embraced him in a bear hug, and kissed his cheeks three times.

"Misha! Thanks for seeing me on such short notice." Gorshkov smiled and said, "Please be seated."

Ryzhkov sat on a sofa facing the prime minister, who sat behind a large oak desk.

"Did you get the information?" Gorshkov asked.

"Ferrari has provided us with the names of those responsible for destroying our Saudi operation."

"What do you propose?" asked Gorshkov.

"The key operatives were Mark Ericksen, Lars Wahlberg, Fico Delgado, Kate McDonald, and Hans Christian Scharz."

"Leave the Swiss federal police officer off the list. Too many of our friends have their money in Swiss banks."

"Let me add Sullivan's name to the list since the bastard directed the operation."

"Sasha, are you mad? We don't want to start a war killing the American secretary of defense."

"Alright, but let me wait until he retires from government," said Ryzhkov.

"Do not push the issue on Sullivan. That's an order!" Ryzhkov's lips tightened into a scowl.

"How do you propose killing them?" asked Gorshkov.

"There are only three left: Ericksen, Wahlberg, and McDonald. I will have our German agent, Heinrich Schroeder, touch base with the Iranian intelligence agency to contract Hezbollah for the hits."

"Once you meet with Schroeder, said a sterned-faced Gorshkov, coordinate the dates and places with Sokurov. There must not be any visible footprints leading back to the Kremlin. Is that clear?"

"Yes, sir."

"You and I both know our economy is dependent on the world market price of oil! We came awfully close to accomplishing our mission, only to have the Americans mess it up!"

"We'll put together a new operation next year," Ryzhkov said.

"We'll wait and see. The presidential elections are coming up next year, and we must make sure that since I'm running for president, we have the support of the oligarchs."

"I'll make sure they are with us or else!" said Ryzhkov.

"Winning the presidency is critical for Russia's future. We must gain more influence in the Middle East and re-capture some of the countries we lost during the breakup. On another topic, I want to congratulate you on your company's innovative strategies, and increased profitability."

"Misha, thanks to you for giving me this golden opportunity."

"I never forget my good friends, especially you. You are one of my best friends. When we have more time, let us plan on going to my estate on the Black Sea with our wives, or would you prefer our mistresses?"

Ryzhkov shook his head and smiled. "Misha, definitely our mistresses."

They stood and hugged, then Ryzhkov left the office. Gorshkov picked up his phone: "Send the director in."

"Yes, sir."

Ten minutes later, the director of the SVR entered.

Over the next fifteen minutes, Gorshkov explained the operation Ryzhkov was managing for him.

"Once I get his plans, I'll provide all the details. I want you and your operatives to monitor all activity and report back to me without his knowledge. Is that clear?"

"Understood, Mr. Prime Minister."

Gorshkov thought about the first time he met Secretary of Defense Sullivan. It was the winter of 1996, and they were both at a diplomatic party hosted by the British Ambassador. Gorshkov enjoyed his meetings at social events with Sullivan. His alias at the time was Wade Davis. Sullivan's official title was economics officer at the US embassy and spoke Russian.

Gorshkov never knew for certain if Sullivan was even a CIA officer, yet alone the station chief. He suspected that most of the Americans employed at the embassy were spies. However, he did learn in 2003, when Sullivan's photo appeared next to President Ridgeway, his title was director of the CIA's counterterrorism center. Gorshkov had fond memories of Sullivan, who struck him as a highly intelligent and engaging person to talk to at these functions.

MOSCOW, METROPOLE HOTEL

On April 1, Heinrich Schroeder and his son Otto arrived at Moscow's Domodedovo International Airport 5:05 pm. The bald Schroeder stood five-eight and was of medium weight. He had a pepper-gray beard, a bulbous nose, red cheeks, and small, mousy brown eyes. At sixty-two years of age, he was the CEO of an industrial company in Hanau, Germany, a Frankfurt suburb. His son Otto was the executive vice-president and chief operations officer. Heinrich Schroeder's company has been doing business for thirty years with Iran, exporting dual-use biological and chemical agents the Iranian Ministry of Defense quietly used to make biological and chemical warfare.

A Mercedes limo driver met him in the hall outside security and drove them to the Metropole Hotel. After checking in to the Metropole Suite on the sixth floor, the telephone rang. He picked it up. "Hello."

"Herr Schroeder, this is Alexander," he said in German. "I'm in the Ambassador Suite. Please come up."

Over the next two hours, they enjoyed dinner and vodka as they discussed the Iranians' proposed meeting.

"Under no circumstances are you to disclose the source of the money or any linkage to the Kremlin," said Ryzhkov.

"Of course not!"

"Once you have reserved a hotel for the meetings, provide me the names of those attending."

"Confirmed," said Schroeder.

Chapter Five

On Tuesday, April 5, Ericksen arrived in Copenhagen on a SAS flight. He and Jeb Templeton, his senior vice-president of marketing, took a taxi to the 5-star Angleterre Hotel on Kongens Nytorv 34. Later that afternoon, they went for a jog around the city.

Four days earlier, they had consummated purchase orders for $3 million worth of EyeD4 systems from the British Ministry of Interior, MI5, MI6, and GCHQ, and a $5 million order from the German Ministry of Interior and the BND (German Foreign Intelligence Service).

At seven-thirty in the evening, Ericksen and Templeton arrived at the Geranium restaurant. Their Scandinavian distributor's managing director and senior managers from Norway, Sweden, Denmark, and Finland were at the bar having drinks when he and Templeton entered.

Ericksen appointed *Amundsen Security Group* in February 2010 to be their Scandinavian distributors. They were based in Oslo, and had established branch offices in Copenhagen, Stockholm, and Helsinki. Thomas Andersen was the managing director of the company. He had the good fortune of meeting Ericksen when they were both involved in *Task Force K-Bar.*

Ericksen commanded a platoon consisting of International Security Assistance Forces from the Australian SAS, Norwegian Forsvarets Spesialkommando, and the Danish Jaegerkorpset. Andersen was a lieutenant and second-in-command under Ericksen. They were involved from the end of December 2001through March 2002 in *Operation Enduring Freedom* in Afghanistan.

The men sat around a large table. During the evening, they enjoyed fabulous entrees and drank beer. Andersen turned his glance at Ericksen and spoke, "Over the past year, we targeted our energies on our primary objectives: ministries of defense and interior, intelligence agencies, defense and aerospace corporations, nuclear power plants, banks, and financial institutions. As of March 31, we have generated $3 million and are expecting an additional $4 million by the end of this year."

Templeton replied, "We are appreciative of your hard work, and we'll support you in your efforts."

Ericksen stood and raised his Tuborg beer glass, "We are confident your company will deliver excellent results for *EyeD4 Systems*."

The men stood and raised their beer glasses. Everyone gave a hearty "Skoal!"

Chapter Six

SCHLOSS HOTEL KRONBERG, TAUNUS, GERMANY

Schroeder planned for the conference to be at Schloss Hotel Kronberg, which had an eighteen-hole golf course on its property. The hotel was formerly a castle built for German Empress Victoria around 1890. It was near Frankfurt.

Schroeder welcomed the Iranian Intelligence Director Esmail Beheshti, his chief of staff Hamid Aghajani, and Iranian Revolutionary Guard Commander Reza Nabavi. They sat around a conference table in the Blue Salon with Schroeder and the intelligence chief.

"Gentlemen, Schroeder said and stood up. I called this meeting because it is of critical importance." He passed three envelopes to each man.

"Please open the envelopes. Look at the pictures of these three Americans: Mark Ericksen, Kate McDonald, and Lars Wahlberg. They all reside in Portland, Oregon. McDonald lives with Ericksen. We will pay $3 million for this operation. We need you to contract with Hezbollah's top operatives to terminate them."

"When do you need this operation completed?" asked Beheshti.

"Within ninety days from today. We will wire the money to your numbered bank account in Liechtenstein, $1 million upfront and the balance when the operation is over."

The Revolutionary Guard commander turned to him and asked, "Can you tell us what these spies did?"

"No."

Nabavi smiled. "It will be an honor to help you."

In another room on the second floor, Sorokin assigned two of his associates to do surveillance on the other two Iranians, and he would follow Aghajani. The SVR also conduct surveillance on the Iranians without Sorokin's knowledge. SVR's Igor Turgenev, a Lt. Colonel at the Russian Embassy in Switzerland, watched Sorokin. Turgenev stood 6'5" and had a very muscular build. Turgenev was from St. Petersburg. He graduated from Moscow State University in international relations and was fluent in German and English. Turgenev served as a Spetsnaz officer and five years later was recruited by Gorshkov, who at the time was head of the Russian Federation's domestic intelligence service. For the past eleven years Turgenev served in the SVR.

Later that evening, Aghajani took a taxi to an internet café in downtown Frankfurt. He walked in and selected a computer. Sorokin brought along a cyber warfare team to monitor their cell phone communication employing top-notch technology.

Aghajani sent an email to Pelletier Joailliers, Gstaad, Switzerland that read:

"Hello Pierre, please order me the gold bracelet for my wife with the inscription 'Shirin, With Love, Hamid.' This is the one you quoted me at five-thousand francs. Please have it ready for me on April Fourteenth. Hamid."

Sorokin sat at another computer station and was able to intercept the email. After sending it, Aghajani paid the assistant in euros and took a taxi back to the hotel.

BAUR AU LAC HOTEL, ZURICH

On April 13, Reza Nabavi held a meeting at the Baur Au Lac Hotel, an elegant five-star hotel catering to kings, dictators, prime ministers, presidents, diplomats, movie stars, business leaders, and wealthy tourists.

In a deluxe suite with a view of the lake and seated around a living room table were high-ranking officers of the Iranian government and their proxy: Reza Nabavi, commander of the Iranian Revolutionary Guard; Esmail Beheshti and his chief-of-staff, Hamid Aghajani, Ismail Al-Musawi, Hezbollah military commander; and Samir Hakim, Hezbollah Secret Service.

Nabavi placed two envelopes in front of Hakim and Al-Musawi. Speaking in Arabic, he said: "These are photos of two American men and one American woman to be terminated: Mark Ericksen, CEO of *EyeD4 Systems*, in Wilsonville, Oregon; and executive vice-president and COO Lars Wahlberg. Also included is a photo of Kate McDonald, who lives with Ericksen. In the envelope you will also find information on their home and company addresses. We will provide you with $1 million down and the balance when you've completed the operation."

Ismail Al-Musawi was a protégé of Imad Mughniyah, Hezbollah's most exceptional and now-deceased terrorist leader. The world media claimed it was a CIA-Mossad bombing that killed him in Syria in 2008.

"It would be an honor to accept this operation. What is the time-line for this operation?"

Nabavi turned to both Hezbollah men. "They all must die no later than July 30."

"We will plan on arriving in Oregon the third week of May," said Al-Musawi.

Later that evening, Aghajani finished his dinner in the suite, stood up, and said to Beheshti in Farsi, "My wife and I are leaving tomorrow for a week of skiing in Gstaad. I'll be back in Tehran on Friday, the 21st."

"Hamid, have a great time, and don't break any bones."

Aghajani did not intend to spend an inordinate amount of time skiing and possibly breaking some bones. He was going to Gstaad to personally pass a critically important message to his old college friend, Yossi Roubini. They both graduated from the University of Washington in 1990 with B.S. degrees in business administration.

After dinner, he and his wife took out some reading materials. While she was reading a romance novel, he sat on the couch in the suite and thought about his friend, Yossi Roubini. In September 1988, Aghajani met Roubini for the first time. Roubini joined a soccer team that played on Sundays. Aghajani was five-foot-ten, weighed 160 pounds, and played center midfielder. The muscularly built Roubini stood six-foot-one, weighed 180 pounds, and played goalie for the other team. Over the next several weeks of playing, they got to know each other. They both spoke Farci, but when he learned Roubini was a Persian Jew from Israel, he kept their friendship at a distance. There were no discussions about politics. They focused their interest on college courses and soccer.

Roubini had dark brown curly hair and sparkling brown eyes. His face bore a two-inch scar running over his left brow, and his nose was broken. He was born in Tehran, Iran, in 1963, and his family left Iran for Israel in 1975. When he graduated from high school, he entered the Israeli Defense Forces. After five years of service, he reached the rank of captain and left the Sayeret Matkal, Delta Force's Israeli version. In 1986, he was accepted at the University of Washington.

In June 1990, a few days after graduation, Roubini met with Aghajani on the evening before his flight back to Israel. He told him if he ever visited England and wanted to get together with him, please get in touch with my uncle. His name is Moishe Roubini, and he owns a jewelry store named *The Gold Palace* in the Knightsbridge section of London. I will let my uncle know about you and advise him to call me when you are in London. Since our countries are adversaries, it would be best for you to call his store with a burner phone.

Over the next several years, Aghajani acquired an MBA from the American University of Beirut and gained proficiency in the Arabic language. In 1995, he was working on his doctorate at Cambridge University. He thought about Roubini, and on his next visit to London, went to *The Gold Palace* on Brompton Road in Knightsbridge. He met Roubini's uncle Moishe, and speaking in Farci, introduced himself as a friend of Yossi's. He gave Moishe his burner cell phone number and his address in Cambridge and asked him to have Yossi contact him. The uncle remembered his nephew mentioned Hamid Aghajani as a good college friend from Iran. Moishe gave him his private telephone number too.

Three weeks later, Aghajani took the train to London and booked a hotel room in the Knightsbridge area. He entered the jewelry store, saw his friend Roubini, and they took a cab to the suburb. After entering a pub, having several beers and a sandwich, they talked about their careers. Roubini mentioned after he left the states, he enrolled at Tel Aviv University and received an MBA. For the past three years he worked as a marketing manager for an Israeli defense contractor. They were careful not to discuss their countries' political situation, and Aghajani always thought Roubini could be an Israeli spy.

After Aghajani received his Ph.D. in international relations from Cambridge, he was in high demand for more significant Iranian government opportunities. He joined the Iran National Oil Company in 1997, and spent several years brokering deals with China and Japan. In 2002, the Iranian Ministry of Foreign Affairs appointed him to an advisory position reporting to the Iranian Foreign Affairs minister. By this time, he was married with two young daughters. He was getting tired of government bureaucracy and, in 2005, became a professor of international relations and management at the University of Tehran. In 2007-2009, Iran had massive fuel shortages that spiked riots, burned gas stations, and arrested many people.

In the 2009 Iranian presidential election between the current president and the progressive opposition candidates, protests erupted all over Iran. Students were rioting, and many innocent people were arrested, shot, and killed. During this unrestful period, the Iranian Minister of Intelligence desperately needed an intelligent, highly experienced, and loyal chief of staff to Iran's Islamic Republic.

The name that kept surfacing among the leading candidates was Hamid Aghajani. He was offered the position, but he was turning sour on the Iranian regime by this time. He personally could not stand the riots of 2007 and 2008, nor the hundreds of students and civilians who were shot, arrested, tortured, and or killed. Aghajani knew he could not say no without having significant suspicion drawn over him. Furthermore, his wife's father was a member of the Iranian parliament and a former military general. It was during this time he needed to get in touch with his old college friend Roubini.

While on a trip to Paris in 2009, he picked up a burner phone, called *The Gold Palace* and asked for Moishe Roubini. He told him he needed to get in touch with his nephew immediately. He left his burner phone number and asked if Yossi could call him back at eleven pm the following night.

A day later, Yossi Roubini called his burner phone.

"I'm now working as a commercial counselor at the Israeli Embassy in Berlin. Is there a chance you could meet me in Zurich within the next two weeks?"

"I'll try and set something up."

"I'm calling your burner phone from my burner phone. Call me once you set up your trip."

"Great!"

Two weeks later, Aghajani arrived in Zurich. He called Roubini's burner phone.

"Hamid, take the Zurich passenger ship BAT 3730 at 11:20 am at the Zurich Burkliplatz. When you arrive at Kusnacht, get off and take a cab to the rail station. Once you arrive at the rail station, walk two blocks to Bergdorf's Café and look for a white BMW. When you see me, jump in. I'll drive back to the Seehotel Sonne at Kusnacht, park the car, and we can have lunch in my room," said Yossi.

During the lunch, Roubini provided him with Pierre's email at Pelletier Joailliers in Gstaad. "If there are any Iranian threats directly or through their terrorist organizations regarding Europe, America, or Israel, please email Pierre and write:

'Hello Pierre, please order me the gold bracelet for my wife with the inscription 'Shirin, With Love, Hamid.' This is the one you quoted me at five-thousand francs."

"Thanks, Yossi."

"Be careful, my good friend. Just a word of caution, there was a man following you on foot when you got in my rental car."

"I know. They are always watching me."

Aghajani left the room and took a taxi back to the train station for the trip to Zurich. Roubini did not have to tell his friend too much about the jeweler. Pierre was an Israeli asset and worked with the Mossad.

GSTAAD, SWITZERLAND

On April 14, Aghajani and his wife checked into the Chateau Rosenberg Hotel. He checked his burner phone and noticed a text message: "Meet me at Berghaus Wispile Restaurant at 11:15 tomorrow. Yossi."

On the fifteenth, wearing a blue ski parka, black ski pants, goggles, and a ski hat, he and his wife skied for two hours in the morning before telling her he needed to meet someone at a restaurant. He took the gondola up to the Berghaus Wispile, a mountain restaurant hut almost six thousand feet in altitude.

He entered the restaurant and spotted Roubini seated at a table. Aghajani was now in his early forties, and Roubini was forty-eight. He walked over to the table and shook Roubini's hand. He spoke in Farsi. "Good to see you. It's been close to two years since we last met."

During the lunch, he gave Roubini a thumb drive.

"Ismail Al-Musawi and Samir Hakim have been contracted to kill three former CIA operatives who now work in Portland, Oregon. Everything about the operation is on the thumb drive."

"Hamid, our government has been looking for those two Hezbollah terrorists for over ten years. They have killed several of our operatives and many innocent civilians. Hezbollah's most wanted terrorist Imad Mughniyah trained them."

Aghajani shook his head, "I am sick of my government's support for Assad, Hezbollah, and Hamas. Since the overthrow of the Shah, our country has become one of the world's leading terrorist nations."

"I appreciate your help, but you're taking a major risk in helping us…Roubini put his hand on his shoulder. Be careful, my dear friend, because if you don't already know, I'm with the Mossad."

"Yossi, I've always figured you were with the Israeli Intelligence Service."

They both smiled and laughed.

After lunch, they stood and hugged each other, put their skis on, and skied down different runs. What Aghajani did not know was his friend was also one of Mossad's best assassins.

Chapter Seven

PACIFIC CITY, OREGON

On April 28, Ericksen rented a four-bedroom, three-bathroom home on the beach in Pacific City, Oregon. He, McDonald, Lars Wahlberg, Jeb Templeton, and Sofia Kastrup enjoyed a barbeque dinner on the patio. Wahlberg, Templeton, and Kastrup brought their spouses and kids along. The home faced Haystack Rock and Cape Kiwanda, where surfers were enjoying the ten-foot waves.

Earlier in that afternoon, Ericksen, McDonald, and Wahlberg were surfing one hundred yards out, doing floaters, and riding the waves. They spent a few hours enjoying the pleasures at Cape Kiwanda. Watching these three fun-loving surfers enjoying the rip-roaring waves were Wahlberg's wife and kids. Their adventuresome spirit carried a surreal connection to their past shadowy and dangerous operation. Wahlberg had been the Agency's operations chief with the CIA's paramilitary clandestine section, the Special Activities Division at Bagram Air Base, Afghanistan, in 2002, when he met Ericksen, the former Navy SEAL Team-Six officer. Several years later, the CIA tasked them with CIA officer Kate McDonald, in *Operation Avenging Eagles*.

The employees at *EyeD4 Systems* often enjoyed get-togethers with their families on the Oregon Coast and at the annual employee retreat held in July at the Central Oregon mountain resort community of Sunriver, Oregon. Every year around the first week in August, the company's management booked a three-day employee and family members retreat. In the daytime, many families were involved in the following activities: horseback riding, hiking, rafting on the Deschutes river, cycling, swimming, and tennis. Several employees enjoyed playing golf.

The employees and their families got together in the evening for a dinner in one of the resort's major halls. The dinners were catered by the staff at the resort. EyeD4 Systems' agenda included a ninety-minute company presentation, awards for outstanding performance, and a forecast of the future. Entertainment followed the awards presentation. This included a band and dancing.

LAKE OSWEGO, OREGON

On Thursday, May 12, a caterer prepared the dinner at Lars Wahlberg's home on Wembly Park Road in Lake Oswego, to celebrate Mark Ericksen and Kate McDonald's upcoming wedding. Seated around their large dining room table were Lars Wahlberg and his wife Heather; Bill Sullivan and his wife; Kate McDonald; Mark Ericksen's best man Jeb Templeton; Jeb's wife; McDonald's brother and mother; and finally, Ericksen's mother, father, sister, and her husband. McDonald's brother would have the honor of walking her down the aisle. Their father had passed away five years earlier.

In January, Bill Sullivan had been appointed the secretary of defense by President Porterfield. He looked around the dining room, lifted his wine glass, focused his gaze at Ericksen and McDonald, and said, "We're delighted to celebrate your wedding."

"We're just happy to have you and your wife join us in our celebration," said Ericksen.

McDonald raised her glass and glanced all around the dining room table. "I would like to make a toast to Bill. Thanks for introducing me to Mark."

They all raised their glass for a toast.

"Where are you staying in Maui on your honeymoon?" Sullivan asked.

"We're staying at the Grand Wailea," said Ericksen. Sullivan smiled. "Sounds great!"

Sullivan had been the CIA director during *Operation Avenging Eagles*. He was very fond of both Ericksen and his fiancée. He marveled at how well they looked, happy and full of life. The odds of these two top CIA operatives surviving the dangerous obstacles they faced were remarkable. Ericksen survived a hotel bombing in Hurghada, Egypt, and later was captured, beaten, and tortured by the terrorist mastermind Khalid Al-Bustani before being rescued by Navy SEALS. McDonald was beaten and tortured by Russian arms dealers before being rescued by Ericksen.

WEST LINN, OREGON

On Friday, May 13, the rehearsal dinner was held at the private Oregon Golf Club in West Linn, with beautiful views of Mt. Hood and the Cascade mountain range. Ericksen joined the luxurious golf club in 2008 and conducted several company business meetings there. Ericksen and McDonald stood and raised their glasses for a toast. He looked at his bride-to-be, smiled, and said, "Skoal. I love you."

"McDonald looked straight into his eyes, smiled, and said, "I love you too."

The Ericksen wedding ceremony began at the Oregon Golf Club's Rose Garden on Saturday at 4:00 pm. In the event the weather might change, the wedding planner had rented a large tent over the Rose Garden. The guests to the wedding started arriving at 3:30. People began taking their seats while the musicians played.

Poul Kastrup and his wife, their daughter Sofia and her husband, relatives, and friends of the bride and groom took their seats. Several government security operatives sat at different locations.

At 4:00 pm sharp, Ericksen dressed in a Kenneth Cole black tux, walked down the aisle to the music of "Ode to Joy by Beethoven," and stopped when he reached the small stage platform. The Protestant pastor met him, shook his hand, and turned to face the crowd.

The "Ode to Joy" continued as Kate's mother and an usher strolled down the aisle, where she met Ericksen. She hugged him and then took a seat in the first row, followed by Ericksen's mom and dad. Then Kate's maid-of-honor and her bridesmaids walked down the aisle. The bridesmaids were all dressed in elegant peach-colored gowns. Ericksen's sister and her husband were seated in the third row.

Ericksen's best man, Jeb Templeton, walked down the aisle followed by Lars Wahlberg and the groomsmen. The groomsmen's attire came from the Men's Wearhouse.

Floral arrangements lined both sides of the aisle. Then a pause, as the maid-of-honor and the bridesmaids walked down the aisle.

The guests anxiously awaited the bride and her brother's entrance. They finally walked down the aisle to "The Wedding March by Felix Mendelssohn." Everyone stood to view them.

Kate McDonald looked magnificent in her gorgeous Claire Pettibone Romantique wedding gown and a two-tier beaded veil. All eyes were on the beautiful bride as she walked down the aisle with a glowing smile. When she reached Ericksen, both their faces were beaming with big smiles. Her brother shook Ericksen's hand and sat alongside his mom. McDonald held Ericksen's hand as they looked at each other, then faced the pastor. He glanced at the audience, the music stopped, and he began the ceremony.

The bride and groom exchanged personal comments and continued to smile with joy. Templeton presented the rings to the pastor, who blessed them. Ericksen placed the two-carat diamond wedding ring on McDonald's finger, and she in turn placed a gold wedding band on his finger.

The pastor began the wedding vow: "Mark, repeat after me. I, Mark Ericksen, take you, Kate McDonald, to be my wife."

Ericksen repeated those words.

The pastor continued, "To have and to hold from this day forward." Ericksen repeated those words.

The pastor finished with the words "Mark do you take Kate to be your lawful wedded wife?"

"I do."

The pastor turned to McDonald and asked her the same vows and finished with the words, "Kate do you take Mark to be your lawful wedded husband?"

"I do."

The pastor looked at both and said, "I now pronounce you husband and wife." Ericksen looked at her sparkling green eyes and kissed her as, everyone stood up and applauded.

The musicians started playing "Canon in D by Pachelbel," and the bride and groom walked down the aisle, followed by the bridesmaids and groomsmen, relatives, and friends, and strolled into the Rose Pavilion.

Once they entered the Rose Pavilion, Mark and Kate McDonald, the wedding party, and their parents lined up as friends and relatives walked past them, congratulating them, and offering hugs, and handshakes.

Then everyone picked up their name badges with their respective table seating at the large, decorated table. There were about two hundred guests. Waiters began passing out hors d' oeuvres, and there was a bar where people ordered drinks.

The videographer and photographer kept busy taking many videos and pictures.

Guests went to their designated tables.

A few minutes later, people got up in a set order for the buffet. The choices for the entrees were: vegetarian entrée, herb roasted chicken with roasted shallot and whole grain mustard sauce, grilled steelhead with roasted tomato and fennel beurre blanc, and pan roasted halibut with white wine & lemon caper sauce.

Each table had bottles of Stag Leap 2007 Cabernet Sauvignon, Lange Estate Dundee Hills Pinot Noir 2008, and 2009 Bergstrom Chardonnay from Newburg, Oregon.

Twenty minutes later, Ericksen stood and began speaking, "I

would like to take this wonderful opportunity to thank everybody who came here this evening to share in our wedding celebration." Kate stood and hugged her husband.

"Thank you for sharing this happy occasion with us." She lifted her glass of wine, gently touched Ericksen's glass, and said, "cheers." She motioned to her maid-of-honor to stand.

Sofia Kastrup stood and had a big smile on her face. "Over the past few years, I had the opportunity of getting to know and appreciate the kindness and joy Kate and Mark have given to me and my husband. Working at EyeD4 Systems has provided me a wealth of experience and happiness in being part of a real team." Kastrup raised her wine glass and said, "Please join me in a toast to the happy couple. Cheers." She sat down.

The best man, Jeb Templeton stood. The former Delta Force major surveyed the room. "I am honored to be the best man for my dear friend and former Navy SEAL Mark Ericksen. I am lucky to be standing here today because nine years ago, our team was on a dangerous mission in Afghanistan, and I was gravely wounded. Mark saved my life!" He raised his wine glass, and continued, "Please share with me this special moment and toast my wonderful friends, Kate and Mark." Everyone was moved by Templeton's speech. Many people stood and said, "Cheers."

Twenty minutes later, the wedding cake was rolled in for the cutting of the cake.

The festivities continued with a slide show of key events in the lives of McDonald and Ericksen. Photos of Kate McDonald appeared chronologically from a cute baby to a five-year-old going to kinder-garten. She took us through the years to her high school and her university graduation at Stanford. Then it was Ericksen's turn, many pictures of him as a child in Denmark, and then playing football and wrestling at Mercer Island High School, becoming an All-American NCAA wrestling champ at Oregon State University, as a Navy SEAL Lieutenant in full battle gear boarding a helicopter.

The groom and bride then danced to "From This Moment" by

Shania Twain. Over the next two hours, people enjoyed the dinner and Dancing. It was a night the happy couple will always remember.

On the fifteenth of May, the honeymooners departed in the morning on a Hawaiian Airlines flight to Maui.

Chapter Eight

On May 19, Roubini was reading *"Bodily Harm"* by Robert Dugoni in his study at his home in Netanya, Israel, when he heard a sound from his secure cell phone. He retrieved a message saying, "The French girls will be arriving on May 24 in Portland, Oregon, and performing at the Ritz on Broadway – Husky."

The text message came from his old friend Aghajani's burner phone, sent from Zurich. *Husky* was the mascot name of the University of Washington, their alma mater.

PORTLAND, OREGON

Al-Musawi arrived in San Francisco under a false French passport with an Algerian surname. He went through customs and transferred to a flight to Portland. Upon arrival at Portland International Airport, he was met by an old friend from Lebanon who fifteen years earlier had immigrated to the United States.

Assassin#1 was about thirty-five years old and had graduated from a local university. He worked for a technology company in Beaverton. Short, with dark black hair, a mustache, and nicely dressed in business casual, he drove Al-Musawi in his Jeep Wrangler to his house in Sherwood, a Portland suburb.

Hakim flew into Chicago under a phony French passport with a Moroccan name and connected to a flight to Portland a few hours later. Assassin#1 met Hakim when he entered the general area and drove him to his house.

Ericksen and McDonald came back on May 22 from Hawaii, relaxed and tanned from their fabulous honeymoon. McDonald told Ericksen she intended to keep her name. Ericksen agreed. They also held a secret: Kate McDonald was three months pregnant.

The Hezbollah team started surveillance on Ericksen's home in West Linn and Wahlberg's home in Lake Oswego. They were trying to gauge times the men left home for the office, to go jogging, or to go to their health club in the morning. Al-Musawi and Hakim were waiting for one more team member on the hit squad to join them. Assassin#2 was from Seattle. He was in his late twenties, tall, medium build, dark black hair and a beard, dressed in Levi jeans, a lumberjack shirt, and sneakers. He drove his Toyota Rav 4x4 to Lake Oswego and registered at the Fairfield Inn.

Assassin#1 observed Ericksen running early in the morning, usually between 5:50 or 6:00 am. During his first several days in Portland, he noticed Ericksen jogged on Tuesday, Thursday, and Saturday. He left his home on Rawhide Drive to Hidden Springs Road and ran down the hill to Mary S. Young State Park off Willamette Drive and back. It was roughly a five-mile run in total.

Roubini arrived at Portland International Airport on a flight from Europe and was met at the airport by a team member who was an American Israeli citizen who worked as a security consultant in the Pacific Northwest. Two Mossad operatives arrived in Portland a few hours later. The common thread they shared with Roubini was their past and he was their commander in Unit 269. They were formerly special forces operators in Sayeret Matkal, the Israeli version of Delta Force.

The Mossad operators' code names were Delta and Omega. They had spent ten years in counterterrorism and the Kidon, the assassination division of Mossad. The Mossad team carried forged British passports. Roubini contacted his former team sergeant from Unit 269 who resided in Oregon and was a naturalized American citizen. His code name was Echo.

Echo lived in Lake Oswego on River Run Drive. He was married, with two children who were away at college. Roubini and team member Delta would stay in Echo's home during the operation. The other team member, Omega, registered at the Crown Plaza in Lake Oswego.

Over the next several days, the assassins became acquainted with the area and conducted surveillance on Ericksen and Wahlberg's movements. Both men worked in Wilsonville. EyeD4 Systems offices on Southwest Parkway Avenue were just a few blocks from FLIR Systems, another defense contractor. The men also drove to Club Sport, an upscale health club in Tualatin, where they worked out two or three days a week when in town.

On Wednesday, June 8, Ericksen was in Wilsonville's Costco Warehouse and noticed an Arab-looking man who appeared to be watching him. It was Al-Musawi. Watching Al-Musawi was Roubini. Ericksen became suspicious of the Arab-looking man, and when Al- Musawi sensed Ericksen's intense alertness, he left the warehouse.

Ericksen then noticed another Arab or Iranian-looking man who briefly stood next to him by the book area. Roubini turned around and glanced at the magazine rack and then went to the check-out line. For a few seconds, Ericksen thought the faces resembled Afghan or Iraqi men from the past.

Roubini's team observed the Hezbollah hit team doing surveillance on both Ericksen and Wahlberg. Omega and Delta followed Al-Musawi. Roubini started using a drone to monitor Ericksen when he left his home. His team also noticed the Hezbollah team following Ericksen from a reasonable distance whenever he left his house. Their vehicles were the same ones used several days in a row.

On June 11, Omega and Delta began parking their rented Honda Odyssey on the street two-hundred feet from the home of assassin#1.

They managed to set up their laser beam technology, which

enabled them to convert the house's sound waves into speech. All Al-Musawi's team met in the living room, where they discussed their daily progress. The window to the living room faced the street.

On Monday, June 13, at 8:30 pm, Al-Musawi and his hit team sat down in the terrorist's home.

"We have established a pattern on Ericksen's runs," Hakim said in Arabic, "which begin around six in the morning, three days a week when in town. Time is running short for us. Let us carry out the operation tomorrow morning."

"You guys take me to Mary S. Young State Park, drop us off at the main parking lot at 6:15 am, and then park in the gravel parking area by the Trillium Trail," said Al-Musawi.

Looking at assassin#2, Al-Musawi said, "You drive your Toyota and park it in front of the trail map area. The timing of the hit will determine which trail Hakim and I take back to one of your cars."

Roubini and his team met at 11:00 pm at Echo's home in Lake Oswego. He felt the first hit would be on Ericksen, and the likely location would be Mary S. Young State Park. They sat around the couch in the great room. Omega and Delta returned to Echo's home and played the recordings. Omega, Delta, Echo, and Roubini heard the tape again for the second time.

He motioned to the men, "Echo and Delta, you two drive into the park, pull-up next to the driver of the Jeep Wrangler by the parking area next to Trillium Trail and kill him. Then go to the dental office in the strip mall and wait. When you receive my call, drive through Mapleton Drive to the park gate and pick me up. Omega, you, drive up to the main parking area near the trail map area and drop me off. Then park and keep a watch on the driver of the Toyota Rav 4x4 with Washington plates," Roubini said in Hebrew.

Echo parked his white Honda CR-V on Suncrest Drive off Hidden Springs Road. Delta sat in the passenger seat. Echo got out of the car, activated his drone to fly over Ericksen's home, got back into the car, and managed the controller. The drone's built-in camera spotted Ericksen running down Carriage Way to Hidden Springs Road, and he immediately called Roubini on his encrypted cell phone.

"He reached Hidden Springs Road and is running down the hill," Echo said in Hebrew. "A Jeep Wrangler just passed him and drove toward Willamette Drive."

Roubini said "Confirmed."

Mary S. Young State Park opened at six. The time was 6:05 am. Omega drove his rented black Honda Odyssey inside the park and dropped off Roubini at the trail map area across from the off-leash pet area. Roubini exited the vehicle dressed in black, sporting a black beard, dark sunglasses, and a cap. There were no cars parked in the parking area. Roubini carried a large backpack and walked six hundred feet down Riverside Loop Trail.

He climbed up a hill surrounded by large douglas fir trees, unpacked his bag, and assembled his semi-automatic Israeli Desert Eagle handgun with a silencer. He placed a clip into his gun.

Ten minutes later, assassin#1 drove his Jeep Wrangler up to the trail center map, and Al-Musawi and Hakim got out. They walked five hundred feet down the Riverside Loop Trail. Assassin#2 arrived at the gravel parking lot near Trillium Trail. He parked, stayed behind the wheel, and rolled the window down eight inches.

Five minutes later, Echo drove his car up with Delta in the front passenger seat and parked thirty feet from assassin#'2's parked vehicle. Echo got out, approached the car, and said in English, "Do you have the time?"

Assassin#2 did not understand what the man was saying and became suspicious. Echo took out his handgun with a silencer and fired two shots through the window opening, killing the man. Then he and Delta drove out of the park.

Al-Musawi hid behind a large fir tree. Hakim stood next to the tree, waiting for Ericksen to jog down the trail.

"Samir, you have a golden opportunity to kill this ex-SEAL with your martial arts expertise," said Al-Musawi.

"I'll split his throat and decapitate the fucking CIA pig," said Hakim.

"Get ready! He's about fifty yards up the hill."

Ericksen saw the dark-haired Arab walking toward him. He intuitively felt the flight-or-fight instinct as he was within ten feet of the assassin. Hakim held his knife in his right hand and suddenly he lunged at Ericksen with his dagger and missed. Ericksen faced Hakim in a martial art pose, led with a left to his neck and a kick to the groin, sending Hakim onto the pavement near the tree. The assault on Hakim knocked away his knife. Al-Musawi came out from behind the douglas fir tree with his Makarov handgun aimed at Ericksen's head.

"Get down on your knees!"

Hakim shook his head, whipped the blood from his nose, and said, "You fucking CIA pig!"

Two shots fired from Roubini's Desert Eagle hit Al-Musawi's right hand and left calf. He immediately hit the pavement. Hakim starred up toward Roubini.

"You Hezbollah scumbags!" Roubini said in Arabic.

Al-Musawi looked puzzled at the man who spoke Arabic to him. "Who are you?"

"I'm your worst nightmare. I can assure both of you of one thing: you're going to die." He leveled his handgun at Hakim's eyes.

Hakim uttered his last words, "Allahu Akbar," as Roubini squeezed off two shots to his forehead.

Two joggers heard the shots near the trail entrance, saw the killer shoot the man, turned, and ran to their cars. The male jogger got behind the wheel while the female jogger called 911 and drove away.

Roubini turned slowly to Al-Musawi and aimed his weapon at his face.

"You're Mossad! You filthy pig!" said Al-Musawi.

Roubini pointed his Desert Eagle at Al-Musawi's eyes, then blasted two shots into his head, and for good measure, two more into his heart.

Ericksen looked at the killer and slowly stood up. "Who are you?"

"Mr. Ericksen, you don't know me, but I'm one of the good guys. Shalom."

Assassin#1 heard muted sounds of gunfire and waited for Al-Musawi's instructions or his appearance. Roubini then called Omega.

"Kill him and then take off."

Omega parked two spaces from the terrorist. He got out of his rented car, walked toward the driver, and held his Sig-Sauer P226 with a silencer. No one was in sight as Omega fired two shots into his head from almost point-blank range.

During the minute it took for the police dispatch to answer the call, Roubini called Echo on his secure cellphone.

"Pick me up on Mapleton Drive next to the park gate." He then called Omega. "Take off now!"

Ericksen walked up to the parking area and waited for the police. Five minutes later, Roubini made it to the park gate, got into Echo's Honda CR-V and drove off.

Ten minutes later, three West Linn police cars and two Clackamas County Sheriffs' Department cars arrived. The officers met Ericksen by the Mary S. Young trail map. Three cops and two deputies carefully walked with their weapons drawn to where the two men had died.

Two West Linn Fire Department ambulances arrived to remove the bodies from the Riverside Loop Trail. The forensics team would begin the process of collecting evidence.

A West Linn police lieutenant and a member of the FBI's Joint Counterterrorism Task Force arrived. All law enforcement teams knew of Mark Ericksen because on July 19, 2009, he had killed two men, Shane Dawkins and the terrorist mastermind Khalid Al-Bustani in his West Linn home. They also knew Ericksen was a former Navy SEAL veteran and a successful defense contractor in Wilsonville, with ties to the intelligence community.

The FBI agent approached Ericksen. "We'll need you to come to the FBI office and give us a full report on everything you know about these murders and the man who executed them."

"I have a few questions for you right now, and then I would like you to show us the actual murder scene. Do you know any of the dead men?"

Ericksen shook his head. "No."

"Do you know who killed them?"

"No."

"Can you describe the killer for us?"

"He's about six-feet-tall, medium build, dressed in black, had a black beard, a mustache, wore a black cap and dark sunglasses. He killed them with a large semi-automatic handgun. He spoke to the men in Arabic."

"Did he speak to you?"

He thought for a brief second and said, "No."

"Where did he go after he killed the men?"

"He ran, turned left, and went uphill on Riverside Loop Trail toward the end of the park."

"Do you have any knowledge about the two other men who were killed in their cars?"

"I didn't know there were other men involved," said Ericksen.

A few minutes later, he received more in-depth questioning. Since this looked more like an assassination with foreign operatives, it would fall under the FBI's authority.

Ericksen walked into the FBI conference office with key people from the West Linn Police Department, Clackamas County Sheriff's Office, Oregon State Police, the FBI Joint Counterterrorism Task Force, and the FBI Hostage Rescue Team.

They asked him more questions for two hours, but he did not divulge any information on the killer because the Israeli operative had saved his life. His country had an excellent relationship with America.

He left with a West Linn police officer who offered to drive him home. Ericksen sat in the back seat and thought for a moment. He needed to immediately check in with Sullivan and share what he knew about the Israeli operative who saved his life.

Chapter Nine

PORTLAND, OREGON

On June 15, *The Oregonian* and other major US newspapers covered the story several hours after the attempted terrorist attack on Ericksen and the mystery surrounding the murder of the terrorists.

The article stated "The murderer and his accomplices are on the loose. The murderer of the two terrorists who attacked Ericksen was a man in his forties, average height, who wore a black shirt, black slacks, black beard, black cap, and dark sunglasses."

Ericksen made a call on his encrypted cell phone to Bill Sullivan, the secretary of defense. Sullivan heard his cell phone ring and picked it up in his office.

"Hello."

"Sir, Ericksen here."

"The FBI director just informed me you were the target of an assassination attempt."

"Fortunately, an Israeli operative saved my life."

"We need to talk in person. I will be out of the country until June 20. Can you be available on the 22nd?" asked Sullivan.

"Yes, sir. I'll be traveling tomorrow to Zurich on business, and I'll change my plans and fly back to Dulles on the 21st."

"One of my staff will get back to you sometime on June 21. We'll need to collect intelligence in the meantime."

Bill Sullivan had graduated from UCLA with a degree in Russian history. After spending four years in the Air Force as an intelligence officer, the CIA recruited him. Sullivan spent close to thirty years with the Agency, including working dangerous assignments like his Special Operations Officer service in Pakistan from 1983-1985. His two-year service from 1995-1997 as CIA station chief at the US Embassy in Moscow gave him a greater perspective on the Russian Federation. Sullivan sensed Ericksen's assassination attempt was tied to the operation he had directed against the terrorist mastermind in 2009.

The next day, Echo left his home early in the morning and drove his car accompanied by Roubini and Delta. He dropped Delta off at the Greyhound bus terminal in Portland. Delta bought a ticket to San Francisco and arrived there the next morning. Then he took a taxi to Burlingame and checked into a room on Airport Way. On Saturday, June 18, Delta left San Francisco International for a twelve-hour flight to London on United Airlines.

Omega called the rental car office where he rented his Honda Odyssey and asked if he could drop the vehicle off in Seattle on June 20. He made his return flight reservations for Tuesday, June 21. After he dropped off his rental car in Seattle, he checked into a Seattle International Airport hotel. The next day he departed to London on British Airways.

Echo and Roubini continued on I-5 to California and arrived in San Jose later that evening. They booked two rooms at the Holiday Inn. The next day, Echo dropped off Roubini at the Greyhound terminal where he bought a bus ticket for Los Angeles.

When he arrived in Los Angeles, he took a taxi to the JW Marriott in Santa Monica, paid the taxi driver, and waited in the lobby with his small suitcase. He called his cousin and twenty-five minutes later was picked up in a Mercedes Benz. He spent the next four days at his cousin's Bel Air home. On June 22, he departed from LAX to Zurich on Swiss International Airlines.

ALEXANDRIA, VIRGINIA

Ferrari sat comfortably in a sturdy recliner at his Alexandria, Virginia condominium. The former CIA officer took a puff of his Cuban cigar and lifted his glass of Stolichnaya vodka. He heard the news that Ericksen had survived the assassination attempt in Oregon. He also thought about Kate McDonald, who worked for the CIA as a NOC in Switzerland and had just married Ericksen a few months earlier.

Ferrari had heard the Russians knew McDonald was in the CIA but did not know she was part of *Operation Avenging Eagles*. By adding her name to the list, he had put her life in extreme danger.

Chapter Ten

TEHRAN, IRAN

When Al-Musawi did not get back to the Iranian Ministry of Intelligence, his superiors became alarmed. Then a breaking news item splashed on *CNN International:* "Four members of a terrorist hit team were shot dead in West Linn, a suburb of Portland, Oregon. Law enforcement is currently investigating the matter."

The Iranians got together to discuss the situation. The commander of the Iranian Revolutionary Guard Nabavi, the intelligence director Behesti, his chief-of-staff, Hamid Aghajani, and six staff members met in a secured conference room at the Ministry of Intelligence building in Tehran.

The Guard commander pounded on the table, his face flush with anger. "We have a mole within our organizations! How could our operation fail?"

The intelligence chief shook his head. "We'll find the traitor. Now I have the most unpleasant task of contacting Schroeder and telling them the mission failed."

The men discussed monitoring their respective organizations and report back soon. An hour later, he placed a call to Schroeder.

"Herr Schroeder, if you don't already know, our mission failed. All of our operatives are dead"

"What happened?" Schroeder asked in English.

"We believe there is a spy either in our midst or yours."

A few moments later, Schroeder called Ryzhkov and told him the bad news. He immediately called Sorokin.

"The Iranians believe we might have a spy within our organization... Those idiots!" Ryzhkov threw a stainless steel stapler against the wall, breaking it into many pieces.

"General, there were only four of us on our team. You only shared it with Gorshkov's chief-of-staff. I wouldn't be surprised if it were Aghajani, their chief-of-staff," said Sorokin.

"Why do you think it might be him?"

"I kept tabs on him. In the evening, he left the hotel, entered an internet café, and sent an email to Gstaad, Switzerland. One of our hackers told us he contacted a jeweler to pick up a gift for his wife on April 14 in Gstaad."

"I'll relay the info to the Kremlin and apprise Schroeder about our suspicions about Aghajani."

On June 20, the top leadership received a brief email from Schroeder about Aghajani's visit to an internet café near the Inter-Continental Hotel in Frankfurt. The Guard commander did not like Aghajani, and this information fueled his suspicions too. Aghajani's father was a well-respected physician whose many patients were serving in the Iranian government. Also, his father-in-law served in the Iranian Parliament. The Guard commander knew he had to be incredibly careful before taking any executive action.

CIA HEADQUARTERS

On June 22, Defense Secretary Sullivan, the CIA director, the FBI director, Ericksen, and Wahlberg met in a SCIF (sensitive compartmented information facility) on the seventh floor. They spent the next hour going over Ericksen's morning run from his home down to Mary S. Young State Park in West Linn, and the events that had led to his being saved from certain death by the terrorist hit team.

Sullivan was six feet tall, about 175 pounds, lean, athletic, muscular, with hazel eyes and greyish-blonde hair. His hair was well groomed and short. He had a broad forehead, a curved Roman nose, and perfect teeth, noticeable whenever he smiled.

"What did the killer say to the two terrorists?" asked Sullivan.

All eyes were now on Ericksen. "'From my basic Arab language knowledge," he said, 'You rotten Hezbollah scumbags."

"Also, the terrorist leader shouted to the killer something like, 'You're Mossad, you filthy pig!"

"Mark, someone in high places wants you dead," the FBI director said.

"I suspect it has to do with *Operation Avenging Eagles*," said Ericksen.

Sullivan looked intently at the FBI director. "I will be meeting with the defense minister and the Mossad director-general in Israel soon. Hopefully, we'll get more details about their covert mission."

"We'll be interested in your findings," the FBI director said.

Ericksen and Wahlberg spent the evening with Sullivan over dinner in Georgetown. They discussed old times, and the topic changed to the current threats to their lives. Sullivan then told them he would ask the FBI to arrange security arrangements with local enforcement for Ericksen, his wife, and Wahlberg.

ZURICH

On June 28, Aghajani flew to Zurich to meet with his banker. In the afternoon, he called Roubini on his burner cell phone.

"Yossi, should anything happen to me, I want you to know that Shroeder was recently in Moscow and stayed at the Metropole Hotel. I believe the Russians issued the kill orders on Ericksen, McDonald, and Wahlberg. Shroeder gave us $1 million as a down payment and said he would pay the balance when the mission was over."

"I recommend you make plans to get you and your family out immediately, Roubini said. I can help you."

"Since our meeting in Switzerland two months ago, they have increased their surveillance on me."

"Hamid, we have agents in Tehran who can immediately help you get out of the country. You must let me help you before it is too late!"

"Thanks, Yossi. I'll get back to within the week."

TEHRAN

On June 30, Aghajani kissed his wife and his two young children before going to work. While driving to his office in Tehran, a motor-cyclist pulled alongside him at a stoplight and fired three shots into his head, instantly killing him. The motorcyclist sped from the scene.

Chapter Eleven

On Tuesday, July 5, Ryzhkov sat on an antique upholstered chair from Czar Nicholas's old palace. The SVR director occupied one chair, and the FSB director was in another chair.

"Sasha," Gorshkov said, his face flushed red with anger, "I need you to take care of a personal job for me. Igor Kublanov is covertly supporting Chekalov. I've told him to never support any opposition party against me."

"Do you have any date in mind?" asked Ryzhkov.

"As soon as possible."

"Sorokin and I will develop a plan to kill him."

"I don't care how you kill him," Gorshkov said.

"You will not be disappointed, Misha."

"Good. On another issue, what went wrong with the Hezbollah hit team?"

"Somehow, Ericksen managed to overcome the team and neutralized them."

"This former Navy SEAL is a brutal thug. What are you going to do about it?"

"I am planning to involve Wolfgang and our best men," Ryzhkov said. "We won't fail this time."

"When you come back, let's make plans for our visit to Sochi." They smiled, and he left the prime minister's residence.

Ryzhkov took out his cell phone and called Sorokin's number. "Hello," Sorokin answered in Russian.

"Make plane and hotel reservations for us with a departure to London on Thursday, July 8," said Ryzhkov.

LONDON

On Friday, July 8, Ryzhkov and Sorokin registered at the front desk of the Sheraton Hotel in Knightsbridge. They went to their respective hotel rooms. Sorokin took out his burner phone and called Ferrari at his condo in Alexandria. Ferrari picked up.

"Hello."

"This is Gerhard. My boss is interested in your company to represent us in England. Can you be available to meet us in London?"

"It will have to be the first part of September," replied Ferrari.

Ryzhkov took out his cell phone which had a Swiss number, linked to his European operation headquarters in Zug. The landline phone rang at Kublanov's residence in Mayfair at four in the afternoon.

"Hello," a male voice said in Russian.

"May I talk with Igor Vladimirovich Kublanov please," said Ryzhkov in Russian.

The man looked at his caller ID and knew who it was. "Who should I say is calling?"

"Alexander Ryzhkov."

"Please hold General Ryzhkov," Kublanov's chief bodyguard said. He walked by the living room where Kublanov glanced over the *International Herald Tribune*.

"Sir, General Ryzhkov is on the phone for you." He handed the phone to his boss.

"Greetings, Alexander. How are you?"

"I'll be in town Monday and have several meetings until Wednesday. However, I was hoping we could meet for lunch or dinner at a restaurant of your choosing sometime next week, perhaps on Wednesday."

"The thirteenth won't work, but I am free on Thursday. Would you like to join my wife and me for dinner at our home?"

"Thank you, Igor," said Ryzhkov.

"How many are in your party?"

"Just my senior vice-president Viktor Sorokin, my assistant, and me."

"How about arriving around eight in the evening," said Kublanov. "We'll be there."

Sorokin and an aide named Evgeny, a former elite Spetsnaz operative who used the alias Egon, had been conducting surveillance over the past five days on Kublanov. On Thursday, July 14, the Russian went to Hyde Park with his two bodyguards and walked around Serpentine Lake. Hyde Park was about one mile from his home in Mayfair. The time was 2:00 pm. and the temperature was in the low eighties, sunny, with a light breeze.

Kublanov and his bodyguards sat on a bench by the lake. Sorokin was about two hundred yards from them. He was hiding in a row of bushes and removed his AK-47, placed a scope onto the barrel, focused on Kublanov's shirt pocket, aimed, and fired two shots, instantly killing him. The bodyguards were in shock as Evgeny dropped one of them with a perfect headshot. The other tried to flee but was gunned down by Sorokin's next shot to the temple. Blood poured everywhere. Sorokin and Evgeny immediately broke down their AK-47s, removed the scopes, and placed them in their duffel bag.

Three minutes later, both men left the park, jumped into a Mercedes SUV driven by Ryzhkov, and sped away. The killings made the *BBC* and the other major TV networks' breaking news fifteen minutes later.

Chapter Twelve

LONDON

The Metropolitan Police Special Crime and Operations Unit started the homicide investigation into the Russian billionaire Igor Kublanov and his two bodyguards. They interviewed Kublanov's wife, his top aide, and family members for information and potential clues.

Over the past five years, several Russian businessmen and former intelligence operatives were assassinated in the United Kingdom. The main suspects were members of the Kremlin or the prime minister of Russia. Since the Russian billionaire was successful and active in social events, the Metropolitan Police contacted the British Security Services MI5 for assistance.

A team of three sergeants, a forensic detective, and an inspector met at Thames House, MI5 headquarters, for their appointment.

Security escorted them into an office where a man in his early fifties shook their hands. He was of medium height and weight with a full head of reddish hair sprinkled with gray and focused hazel eyes and dressed in a dark blue suit. He introduced himself as Roger Hanley. He took a keen interest in the Kublanov assassination because the victim supported Gorshkov's rival in Russia's upcoming 2012 presidential elections.

The Metropolitan Police team had picked up the bullet fragments and determined the killer or killers had used a high-velocity rifle. They guessed the sniper or snipers were positioned in the high grass across the lake from two hundred meters.

"Mr. Hanley, we have been in touch with the telecom carrier and going through all calls made in the last thirty days," said the police inspector.

"Please give us all the calls made to Kublanov's landline and his mobile phone numbers, and we'll run it through GCHQ, " Hanley said.

"Of course, Mr. Hanley."

Chapter Thirteen

ISRAEL

On July 22, Sullivan's Department of Defense Gulfstream G650 jet arrived at Ben Gurion Airport in Tel Aviv, Israel. He was met by American embassy security staff on the tarmac along with two Israeli intelligence security staff and driven to the King David Hotel in Jerusalem. Later that evening, he met American embassy staff and the American ambassador in preparation for his meeting in two days with the Israeli defense minister.

On July 25, his security detail drove him to the American embassy in Tel Aviv. He was later driven to Herzliya and checked into the Ritz-Carleton Hotel. An hour later, a black Mercedes SUV pulled in front of the driveway of the hotel. The driver got out of the vehicle and opened the door for Sullivan and his American security staff.

As they drove off, a Toyota SUV with two American security personnel inside followed the vehicle. The Mercedes parked in front of a luxurious safe house on Spinoza Street in Herzliya. Spinoza Street's safe house was one of the Office's favorite spots for their allies' intelligence heads to meet. The Office was the term the members of Mossad used for the name of their headquarters.

The Mossad's director-general greeted Defense Secretary Sullivan with a hearty handshake. "Good to see you again, my friend."

Sullivan smiled at the short, bald director. The director-general escorted Sullivan into the study. The security details of both leaders walked into the living room.

Once the door was closed and friendly exchanges were made, Sullivan cut right to the point. "What do you know of the Arab terrorists killed recently in Oregon?"

The head of Mossad pushed his chair forward and placed his hands on the rosewood desk. "Once we received intel from our Iranian asset that two of the most dangerous Hezbollah terrorists, Ismail Al-Musawi and Samir Haim, had taken the assignment to kill Ericksen, McDonald, and Wahlberg, we developed a plan to kill them."

Sullivan's eyes zeroed in on him as he moved his head closer to the desk. "Do you know who hired them?"

The jovial sixty-year-old director-general nodded his head. "A German arms dealer named Heinrich Schroeder paid the Iranians to have the Americans killed. Then the Iranians sub-contracted the work to Hezbollah."

"How sure are you that Schroeder was the person who ordered the contract?"

"We've been conducting surveillance on Shroeder's activities with the Iranians for the past two decades, and we think he was the go-between from someone in Russia, more than likely in the Kremlin," he stated in a serious tone.

"Our case officers in Europe have also been monitoring Herr Schroeder for some time," Sullivan said. "Please provide me with the intel you have on him." He stopped for a moment and motioned with his right hand. "Who killed these two Hezbollah terrorists?"

"One of our best assassins killed them."

"Your operative saved Mark Ericksen's life. Please thank this individual for me."

"We're in a tough business. Good people die from time to time protecting their country. Our Iranian asset was gunned down in Tehran, and our assassin is determined to find the person who ordered the hit and liquidate him."

"If we can be of assistance, please get back to me," Sullivan said.

Lunch followed the meeting, and then the secretary of defense was driven back to the hotel. An hour later, Sullivan went for a forty-five-minute swim in the Mediterranean Sea accompanied by two security guards. He returned to Washington the next day.

Chapter Fourteen

CARMEL, CALIFORNIA

Ericksen and his wife spent the next week looking for homes in the Menlo Park area. The houses in the area were expensive, but after he had killed a terrorist mastermind and a traitor at the end of 2010, the US government had paid him $6 million of reward money. He and his wife decided to take a break and spent the next three days in Carmel. They visited several quaint shops and purchased two seascape paintings from local artists.

In the evening, they went to a restaurant called the Hog's Breath Inn. After a delicious dinner of baby back ribs and two Stella Artois beers, the couple drove back to their hotel, the Ventana Big Sur Resort. They were excited that she was five months pregnant and were looking forward to having a baby girl. She had already registered to have the baby delivered at Lucile Packard Children's Hospital Stanford in Palo Alto.

Their room had a view of the Pacific Ocean. They opened the drapes, opened the window, felt the ocean breeze, and enjoyed the peaceful serenity. They opened a bottle of Stags Leap, and he poured her a little portion of red wine into her glass. They raised their glasses, toasted, and tasted the wine. Their love for each other was strong, and their future looked terrific.

On the second day, Ericksen headed to *On the Beach Surf Shop* on Lighthouse Avenue in Monterey. He met one of his former Navy SEAL buddies who lived nearby and taught at the Naval Post graduate school. Ericksen rented a wetsuit, booties, and a neoprene hood and surfboard. His friend was already in his wetsuit. They placed the surfboards in his friend's pickup and drove to Asilomar State Beach. The waves were at least eight feet tall, and the weather was nice. The only thing to be careful about was the great white sharks. On two occasions two surfers had become victims. The two former SEALs surfed for three hours and then called it a day.

Ericksen and McDonald went to sleep around eleven. About three in the morning, McDonald was tossing around. She bumped into her husband's side and yelled, "You're going to kill me anyway!"

Ericksen shook her and shouted her name until she woke up. Her shivering body was drenched in sweat. "Honey, are you alright?"

"I was having a nightmare about the Russians beating me and holding my head down into the bathtub water. Sergei Ryzhkov ordered me to talk and I told him to go to hell!"

He held her tightly as tears ran down her cheeks. "Honey, take some deep breaths."

"They continued to beat me and finally took me downstairs to the basement."

He continued holding her, as tears ran down his cheeks.

"Honey, the good news is we're alive and they're dead."

McDonald looked into his eyes.

"Mark, I just remembered something. When one of the bodyguards opened the door to the basement, I heard Ryzhkov tell Kupchenko that he was going to Moscow to meet with Sasha."

"Kate, we need to let Sullivan know about Ryzhkov's contact person Sasha. Perhaps this guy in Moscow is the leader."

MENLO PARK, CALIFORNIA

Ericksen and his wife met the realtor in the Palo Alto office and narrowed their search to two homes in the Sharon Heights area of

Menlo Park. On July 28, they selected a 3,100 square foot home on Tioga Drive. The sale would close at the end of August, and they planned to move into their new home on September 1.

After signing the papers, the couple celebrated their new home purchase with a dinner with the CEO, Poul Kastrup, at the Rosewood Sand Hill Hotel in Menlo Park on Sand Hill Road. The men raised their glasses of wine, while McDonald raised her glass of water. Kastrup then raised his wine glass again and looked at Ericksen and McDonald.

"Congratulations on the good news of welcoming a baby soon."

McDonald smiled and said, "Thank you, Mr. Kastrup. We also found a lovely home on Tioga Road in Sharon Heights."

"Mark, you're about ten minutes from the office. Kastrup looked at McDonald. "What are your plans after the baby arrives?"

She looked at Kastrup and said, "Perhaps after the baby is a year old, I will place her in childcare. Then I can plan to review wealth management positions in the banking and financial sectors."

"We'll help you when you're ready."

"Thank you, Mr. Kastrup."

Chapter Fifteen

Sullivan picked up his landline at the Pentagon.

"Sir, you have a call from Mark Ericksen."

"Put him through."

"Yes, sir."

"What's new, Mark?"

"I would have called earlier, but I was told you were on vacation and later in Asia on government business. Everything is going well, except Kate had one of those nightmares at the end of July. She said it unlocked a memory: when the bodyguards were bringing her down to the basement, she heard Sergei Ryzhkov tell Oleg Kupchenko that he had to go to Moscow to talk with Sasha. We hope you can check through your connections if they know anything about a person linked to Ryzhkov or Kupchenko."

"Perhaps this Sasha character is another arms dealer tied to the Russian mafia or the Kremlin. Anyway, we will check it out. Please give my best to Kate."

"I will, sir."

A few hours later, Sullivan met with the director of the CIA in Langley, Virginia. He passed on the information Ericksen had relayed to him about Sergei Ryzhkov's trip to Moscow to meet with

Sasha. The CIA director confirmed she would have her Moscow chief-of-station and her European allies' intelligence chiefs check it out.

LONDON

On September 2, Ferrari drank a vodka shot at the Holiday Crown Express in Hounslow when his burner cell phone on the nightstand started ringing. He lifted the cell phone to his ear.

"Hello Wolfgang," said Ryzhkov calmly. "I'm downstairs in the lobby. What is your room number?"

"308."

Ryzhkov knew Ferrari was the right person to coordinate the mission with his Russian assassins. He was aware that Ferrari was deeply in debt and had gone through a nasty divorce in 2008. He remembered the FSB had conducted surveillance and bugged Ferrari's apartment in Moscow in 2007. The audio they heard on numerous occasions consisted of violent arguments and Ferrari assaulting his wife. The FSB took pictures of his wife leaving the apartment the next day with a black eye and bruises on her forehead. Shortly after that, his wife left Russia with their son for the States. Ryzhkov put his Swiss-registered cell phone back into his pocket and took the elevator to the third floor.

He activated his stealth cell phone recorder as the elevator sped to the third floor. Ryzhkov walked down the hall and approached room 308 and knocked on the door. Ferrari opened the door to greet him and said in English, "Hello, Alexander."

Ryzhkov entered and sat down on the couch. "You probably heard about the attack on Ericksen in Portland. The hitmen were killed by Ericksen and one or two friends of his."

"Yes, of course."

"Ericksen, Wahlberg, and McDonald must die! I can offer you $3 million for this task. I will immediately wire transfer $1 million into your private numbered account in Monte Carlo as a down payment.

You will collect one million dollars each time you kill a remaining

CIA spy. Sorokin will assist you on this mission with two of his best assassins. Are you interested?"

Ferrari became silent for a few moments. His face shifted to the left and then to the right. This mission would be hazardous now that Ericksen, Wahlberg, and McDonald had been alerted. Accepting this deal and being a party to killing three Americans on a CIA operation would seal his fate to a life sentence or even a death sentence. He just could not do it.

He looked directly at Ryzhkov and said, "I can't be involved in killing Americans."

"Tony, have you forgotten? You already are involved! By giving us the names of the *Operation Avenging Eagles* team, you switched your loyalties to us!"

Ferrari shook his head but realized the oligarch had a point, and he knew right then and there the Russian would blackmail him if he did not play ball.

Ryzhkov smiled, "Relax, Tony. All you have to do is plan and coordinate the time and place. Sorokin and his associates will execute Ericksen, his wife, and Wahlberg."

Ferrari knew he needed to accept this operation. Otherwise, his identity would be exposed or worst case, the Russians would kill him. Besides, he desperately needed the money.

"The planning might take six months or longer before it could go operational," Ferrari said.

"You will set up and coordinate the plan with Sorokin. He and his men will poison Ericksen, his wife, and Wahlberg. I'll give you one year from today to accomplish this action."

His eyes met Ferrari with intensity. "Alexander, we have a deal."

Ryzhkov reached into his sport jacket pocket and retrieved a business card with Sorokin's email address. It listed the name of the company as *Ryzhkov and Dorfmann Energy*, Berlin, Germany. His Berlin cellphone number was 49-30-41960.

The German company was a subsidiary of Ryzhkov's holding company. Any emails sent to Sorokin, alias Gerhard, would be forwarded to Ryzhkov's headquarters in Moscow to the attention of

Viktor Sorokin. Ferrari reached to shake his hand, then stood up and left.

Later that evening, someone knocked on his hotel room door. He opened the door and saw a beautiful blonde, green-eyed woman of twenty-five smiling at him.

"Wolfgang, my name is Galina. Gerhard thought you might wish to enjoy my company tonight," she said in heavily accented English.

Ferrari escorted the Russian beauty into his room. "Let us start with some vodka to whet our appetites," he said, grinning. "Then we can discuss the first thing that comes up."

Chapter Sixteen

ALEXANDRIA, VIRGINIA

When Ferrari had worked as the CIA chief-of-station at the U.S. Embassy in Bern, he did not know that Wahlberg, using the alias Dave Jacobson, was involved in *Operation Avenging Eagles*. Wahlberg served under the U.S. Treasury Department's Counterterrorism and Financial Intelligence Division as an economics counselor and was on loan from the CIA. When McDonald, using her alias as Elizabeth Caldwell, was abducted by the Russian arms dealers, he ordered CIA officers to assist Ericksen and Delgado in rescuing her. Ferrari had felt that the CIA did not appreciate his value since the time he was a senior political attaché at the U.S. embassy in Moscow from 2007-2008 until he retired. It probably started with his wife leaving him in Moscow and taking their son with her.

He began drinking heavily and consorted with Russian prostitutes who probably passed information to the FSB. He blamed Bill Sullivan when he was the CIA director for not accelerating his career advancements.

He called Wahlberg at EyeD4 Systems. "Hello, Wahlberg speaking."

"Hi Lars, this is Tony Ferrari."

"I'll be darn. It's been a while since I've heard your name."

"I've been working as a D.C. consultant for the past year, and I'll be up in Portland next week. If you're in town, do you want to get together for lunch or dinner?"

"Tony, unfortunately, I will be out of town all next week."

"Perhaps another time," said Ferrari.

"Take care."

Chapter Seventeen

THE SAN FRANCISCO BAY AREA

Ferrari finished his consulting work with the Washington, D.C. law firm in October and now was pursuing an opportunity with a private equity firm in Menlo Park. He researched Cyberburst Communications, the company where Ericksen served as a vice-president, and discovered that Feldman Capital Group in Menlo Park owned 20 percent of the private company's shares. He had met Feldman at the NSA to discuss Russia's top-security briefings back in 2001.

He sent a four-page proposal to Feldman two weeks earlier via FedEx mentioning his CIA work history. His recent consulting project with the law firm focused on the aerospace and defense sector. His primary consultancy focused on international risk and business intelligence projects.

When Ferrari flew into San Francisco International Airport on November 7, he reserved a room at the San Mateo Marriott on Amphlett Blvd in San Mateo.

The next day, he drove his rental car up Sand Hill Road in Menlo Park and pulled into the parking lot of Feldman Capital Group. He entered the lobby and informed the receptionist of his appointment.

He knew Feldman was well connected within the defense industry and joining this firm would be financially rewarding.

Feldman had an illustrious career as a colonel in the Air Force, holding positions at missile bases and being a staff member of the Joint Chiefs of Staff at the Pentagon, deputy director of the NSA, and a vice-president of wealth management for Goldman-Sachs. He founded his private equity fund in 2006. Feldman was fifty-seven-years-of-age, had blue eyes, silver gray hair, trim beard, stood six-feet-three, and weighed two-hundred-pounds. He played football in college and still maintained an athletic build for his age.

He looked forward to meeting Ferrari again. He spotted him and greeted him in the lobby.

"Tony, you haven't changed much from the last time I saw you."
"Thanks, Sid, but I gained some weight since our last meeting."

He shook Ferrari's hand and escorted him into his large, elegant office. Adorning his wall was his college graduation degree from the University of Washington and his M.S. in computer engineering from Stanford University. Also displayed were awards and commendations from the Air Force, the Pentagon, and Goldman-Sachs. There were pictures of him with dignitaries and celebrities.

Feldman sat behind his walnut desk, a laptop to his right, and Ferrari was seated in a chair facing him.

"I've read a lot about your firm, and I'm impressed with the portfolio you oversee. I could be an asset in conducting risk and business intelligence for your firm if you're in the market for a consultant with my background."

Feldman picked up the four-page proposal outlining Ferrari's AUF Consulting projects, including Engstrom-Knight Aerospace Corporation.

"Tony, you have an impressive background in this field. Should something open up soon, I'll certainly give you consideration."

"I appreciate your kind words. Let's stay in touch," said Ferrari.

Chapter Eighteen

LUCILE PACKARD CHILDREN'S HOSPITAL AT STANFORD

On November 18, a nurse brought the newborn baby girl into McDonald's maternity room on the third floor of the children's hospital at Stanford. Ericksen entered the room and smiled at his wife as she held their baby girl in her arms. He placed roses on the table. Ericksen and McDonald named the baby Anne Elizabeth Ericksen. They fixed up a lovely room for the newborn child with a beautiful crib, changing table, large chest of drawers, and chest of toys. Starting a family, working as an executive of a multi-billion-dollar defense company in Silicon Valley, and knowing they were targets for assassination occupied his thoughts.

PALO ALTO

Ericksen looked at the picture hanging on the wall in his office. It was a photo of the two on them on their honeymoon on the island of Maui. He stood up, walked toward the picture. Suddenly, his encrypted cell phone rang.

He walked back to his desk and picked it up.

"Mark, Sullivan here. I just received information from the Agency. Sasha is Sergei Ryzhkov's brother, who goes by the name General

Alexander Ryzhkov. He formerly ran the GRU, and one of his best friends is Prime Minister Gorshkov. He awarded Ryzhkov an energy and mining company six years ago. Now the oligarch carries out special projects for Gorshkov. We believe he is responsible for the assassination team's attempt to kill you and perhaps others on our operation."

"Shit! We're probably still on their target list."

"Affirmative We believe Khalid Al-Bustani was not aware of the Russian's ultimate plan in aiding them with nuclear devices. Gorshkov was hoping our two cities would be devastated by the explosions, our government would boycott Saudi's oil and encourage our allies to stop doing business with them."

"What about Al-Bustani's attempt to ship a tactical nuclear warhead with a yield of about eight or ten kilotons on a container ship from Karachi via Jakarta to the Port of Los Angeles? Wasn't Gorshkov involved with that plan too?"

"No, the Russians weren't involved. Once we received intel on that operation, I passed it on to the head of Pakistani intelligence, and they seized the nuclear warhead and arrested the Pakistani scientists."

"Sir, thanks for the information."

"Mark, don't worry, the FBI is watching your back."

Sullivan thought about the only meeting he had had with President Gorshkov when he was CIA director under President Ridgeway. He met him during the G8 summit held in St. Petersburg on July 15-17, 2006. When President Gorshkov learned he was a top-notch handball player, he invited Sullivan to play handball at one of St. Petersburg's best handball courts. They played two vigorous games, each man winning a match. After the games, Gorshkov invited President Ridgeway and Sullivan to dinner in his magnificent home. Sullivan observed how Gorshkov evolved from a critical player in the FSB in 1996 to an autocrat engaged in snuffing out any semblance of governmental reforms or transformation to a Russian form of democracy.

Chapter Nineteen

LONDON

On Friday, November 25, Roger Hanley, the MI5 supervisor of the criminal division, decided to personally interview the chief bodyguard and Kublanov's widow. He called the Metropolitan Police inspector to join him and schedule another visit to Mayfair's Kublanov residence. Over the previous several months, MI5 had received Kublanov's landline and mobile phone numbers from the telecom carrier and GCHQ, the NSA of Great Britain.

When they arrived at the door, the chief bodyguard welcomed the Metropolitan Police inspector and Hanley into the residence. The inspector introduced Hanley to him. He had a servant ask if they would like him to place their topcoats in the front closet. The men agreed and followed the servant to the chief bodyguard.

"We collected all the landline phone and mobile phone number logs made to Kublanov's residence," said the inspector. We listed the dates and where the calls originated from by country. We checked not only your landline but also Mr. Kublanov's mobile phone."

"There were a total number of twenty-seven calls made from July 6-12," Hanley said. "Thirty of them came from the United Kingdom, one from St. Petersburg, three from the United States, one from

Monte Carlo, one from Seychelles, and one from Zug, Switzerland. Can you recall who these people are who called?"

"Gentlemen, the call from St. Petersburg was from one of Chekalov's campaign advisors. Most of the others from the United Kingdom were from his immediate family."

"We traced the numbers in the log" the inspector said, "and we have identified all the phone numbers that called into the residence. Do you know the names of the people he talked with from the United States and Switzerland?"

The chief bodyguard looked away, seemingly uncomfortable with the question. He believed the people from the States and Germany were businessmen.

"Is Tatiana Kublanova available?" asked Hanley.

"Let me see." The chief bodyguard got up and left the front room.

Five minutes later, Kublanov's wife appeared. Kublanova introduced herself to the men and sat down on the sofa. She was a woman about sixty years old, attractive with bleached red hair and blue eyes, and dressed in a conservative looking skirt and blouse.

"We were going over the call logs we traced from the period from July 6-12," the inspector said, "and based on your chief bodyguard's recollection, there doesn't appear to be any concerns he had with those people who tried to reach your husband."

"Ms. Kublanova," Hanley said, "I am concerned with one call your husband received on July 12. It was from a Zug, Switzerland, mobile phone number, 41-41-5536428. Do you know the person who called from this number?"

She hesitated for a few seconds, while the chief bodyguard appeared nervous. "Yes, it was from Alexander Ryzhkov. He was planning on having dinner with us at our home on Thursday, July 14."

"Was he the only one to be joining you and your husband for dinner?"

"No. Mr. Ryzhkov also said his vice-president, Mr. Sorokin, and an assistant would be coming for dinner," she said.

"What was his relationship with your husband?" asked Hanley.

"They did business together. Mr. Ryzhkov is a remarkably successful businessman in Russia."

"Did he call you after he heard your husband was found dead?" said the inspector.

"Yes, he told me he was sorry to hear about about the tragedy and offered to help me in any way."

Hanley stood, and the inspector took the hint that it was time to leave. They stood up and thanked both for their cooperation. The servant gave them their topcoats, and they left the Kublanov residence. They headed for MI5's headquarters at Thames House and went to Hanley's office.

"Ryzhkov was formerly head of the GRU for the Russian Federation. He was using a Swiss mobile phone number, and I wouldn't be surprised if he used a fake Swiss passport when he entered the UK," said Hanley.

"Do you think Ryzhkov had something to do with Kublanov's death?" asked the inspector.

"I don't know. However, as a former director of the Russian military intelligence directorate, he must be on good terms with Gorshkov. We will check with MI6, and you check customs and local hotels to see when Ryzhkov entered and left the UK. We'll also thoroughly check his Swiss mobile phone to see what other numbers he has called from that phone since July 1, 2011."

WASHINGTON, D.C.

At the end of September, the CIA director announced Ken Washington, CIA chief-of-station in London, would be the deputy director of the National Clandestine Services. Ken and his wife moved into the Watergate South Complex at 700 New Hampshire Avenue N.W., on December 1.

Over the next several weeks, they checked for homes on the Zillow website. Their daughter was already staying with relatives in Arlington, Virginia, and attending high school. They hoped to find a lovely 3,000 square foot home in the Arlington area by February 2012.

Chapter Twenty

With Ericksen's recommendation, Mitchell promoted Wahlberg to senior vice-president/general manager/chief operating officer of *Cyberburst Biometrics* (formerly *EyeD4 Systems*). The Board of Directors of *Cyberburst Communications* decided to let *Cyberburst Biometrics* remain there because most of its talented engineering staff enjoyed the Oregon lifestyle and affordability. Wahlberg was seated at his desk when his cell phone rang. He picked it up. "Wahlberg speaking."

"Hi, Lars, Tony Ferrari."

"What's up, Tony?"

"I have a meeting with a potential client tomorrow afternoon at three in Beaverton and was hoping you can join me for an early lunch."

"How about eleven-thirty?" said Wahlberg.

"That will work. Where should I meet you?"

"Meet me at the *Claim Jumper* on Lower Boones Ferry Road in Tualatin," said Wahlberg.

"See you there."

The next day, they arrived at the *Claim Jumper.*

"Congratulations on your new position. I heard *Cyberburst Commu-*

nications hired your old boss Mark Ericksen to a senior marketing management position," Ferrari said.

"He's going to do a fantastic job for them. You probably heard that Kate McDonald is married to Ericksen and just had a baby?" said Wahlberg.

"I'm delighted to hear Kate is doing well."

They both reached for their Heineken beers for a toast and said, "Cheers."

"Tony, tell me about your consulting company."

"My clients' are mostly in the defense business. I've been doing this for a little over a year, but to be honest, I would prefer to work in the corporate world in Silicon Valley as a security director."

"You might want to check with *Cyberburst Communications'* headquarters in Palo Alto. The COO of the company is Logan Mitchell, and he might know of some companies in the area that might be in the market for a person with your experience."

"I would appreciate it if you could mention my name to him," said Ferrari.

"I would be glad to get in touch with him. Please send me your resume, and I'll do the rest."

PALO ALTO

On December 6, Mitchell reviewed Ferrari's resume and met with the corporate security director to discuss contracting with Ferrari through his *AUF Consulting* firm. On the resume, he listed Sid Feldman as a reference.

Since Feldman's company owned 20 percent of *Cyberburst Communications'* shares, it was an easy decision to call him. Mitchell lifted his telephone to his ear and called.

"Hello Sid, it's Logan Mitchell."

"What can I do for you?"

"Do you have a few minutes for me tomorrow or Friday, the eighth?"

"Let me check. Feldman glanced at his laptop and said, "I'm good any time from ten to eleven on the eighth."

"Good. I'll see you at ten on Friday," replied Mitchell.

On Friday, the eighth, Mitchell was seated in a chair facing Feldman, who he had known since 2002 when he worked at the Pentagon and Feldman was with the NSA and they worked on a project together. Mitchell retired from the U.S. Air Force as a two-star general back in 2006. However, in 2004 he became one of Feldman's clients at *Goldman-Sachs*. He handled Mitchell's wealth management portfolio.

Mitchell was recruited in September 2006 by *Cyberburst Communications* as its chief operating officer and moved to the Palo Alto area. In 2007, he recommended to Feldman, now the CEO of *Feldman Capital Group*, a private equity firm in Menlo Park, to invest in the company. *Feldman Capital Group* purchased 20% of *Cyberburst Communications* shares at that time.

"I received a resume today from Anthony Ferrari of *AUF Consulting Group*. One of my key men at *Cyberburst Biometrics* in Oregon speaks highly of him, and he also listed you as a reference. What can you tell me about him?" said Mitchell.

"Tony Ferrari's last position with the CIA was station chief in Switzerland. I have known him for at least ten years, and he is a knowledgeable security professional. I would gladly recommend him." Mitchell smiled and said, "I'll schedule a meeting with him."

He opened his briefcase and took out some papers.

"I would like to discuss with you the possibility of Kastrup selling his shares of the company."

Feldman's eyes opened widely. He moved forward in his seat and placed his hands firmly on the desk.

"Do you know something that I don't know?" asked Feldman sarcastically.

"Kastrup is sixty-five-years-old. I believe he has reached the business world's pinnacle of success. I'm speculating, but if Kastrup was interested in selling his shares of the company, would you be interested in purchasing his shares of stock and the remaining investor shares?" asked Mitchell and smiled.

"*Cyberburst Communications* generated $1.4 billion in sales at the end of the June fiscal year," Feldman said. "Kastrup already holds 35 percent of the shares of the company. Our company holds investments worth about 60 billion dollars. Investor valuation of the company's stock purchase would roughly be about $8 billion. How much stock do you own at present?"

Mitchell turned a few pages of documents and looked at Feldman and replied, "3 percent."

"If any corporation purchased the company," Feldman said "your shares would be worth about $40 million. However, I have not received any indication that Poul Kastrup is interested in selling his company's shares. Have you?" He shrugged his shoulders.

"I've been with the company since 2006. I have five years vested with the company. If Kastrup sold his shares, I am convinced I would be next in line to be the president/CEO, assuming the board of directors agree."

Over the next few days, Mitchell reflected on the reliable recommendations that Feldman and Wahlberg had provided him and decided to meet with Ferrari in Palo Alto.

WASHINGTON, D.C.

Ferrari was back at his condominiun in Alexandria, Virginia during the holidays. He invited his children for dinner, but only his daughter accepted. His son hated him and refused to join them. He and his daughter had a pleasant dinner at The Wharf on King Street. She tried to be civil with him. The children had witnessed over the years the abuse inflicted on their mother. That pain would never go away. They were close to their mother, who remarried a banker last year. Ferrari did not have any steady attachments. He dated from time to time but usually had one-nighters. Now he was planning on commuting between Virginia and the West Coast to accomplish his mission.

On Friday, December 16, Washington placed a call at 11:00 am.

Ferrari's cell phone rang in his condominium, and he picked it up on the third ring.

"Hello."

"Hi Tony, it's Ken Washington. How are you?"

"I'm doing okay and yourself?"

"The Agency appointed me to be the National Clandestine Services deputy director position a few months ago. My wife and I are staying at the Watergate complex while searching for a home in the Arlington area."

"That's great!"

"How is your consulting business going?" asked Washington.

"I completed my consulting project with the law firm in October. Currently, I am searching for a corporate security position or a consulting project in Silicon Valley. The opportunities are looking ripe."

"Do you have time for dinner?"

"My schedule is more or less open right now."

"Are you free Monday night, December 19?" asked Washington. "I'm good."

"Be my guest at the Palm restaurant in Georgetown."

"Sounds great! What time, Ken?"

"How about seven?"

"See you there."

On Monday evening, Washington and Ferrari were sitting at the bar waiting for their table. Washington dressed in a navy blue sports jacket, gray slacks, white shirt, and a blue tie. Ferrari wore a black herringbone sports jacket, black slacks, blue dress shirt, red tie, and black leather Testoni shoes.

They briefed each other over the next ten minutes on family matters, politics, the weather, and other cordial matters at the bar when the maître d' interrupted them. "Please let me take you to your table."

"Thank you," said Ferrari.

After being seated, their waiter appeared, placed two water glasses down, and provided them with menus.

"Thank you," said Washington.

"Anything new at the Agency?"

"Well, the last time we met we were concerned about Kublanov's life because he supported Prime Minister Gorshkov's rival, Mr. Chekalov. Well, you probably heard assassins killed Kublanov and his bodyguards in Hyde Park in July."

Ferrari shook his head. "Did they ever find who killed them?"

"No, but MI5 is investigating. They believe it was an assassination ordered by the Kremlin or Gorshkov directly."

Washington lifted his scotch glass and Ferrari raised his vodka.

They gently touched each other's glasses and said, "Cheers."

They glanced at their menus. A minute or two later, the waiter approached. "Gentlemen, are you ready to order?"

Washington looked up with a smile. "I'll have the crab cocktail appetizer and the center-cut filet mignon."

"Good choice. I'll do the same," said Ferrari.

They continued to talk about their families and life in general. When they finished their meals, Washington paid the waiter and left the restaurant. Before going to their respective cars, Ken said,

"Tony, I wish you and your family a Merry Christmas."

"Yours, too, buddy."

PALO ALTO

On January 4, 2012, Mitchell spent two hours talking with Ferrari and appointed *AUF Consulting* for a six-month contract. He outlined several critical areas where Ferrari's firm could help the corporate security director and work with various subsidiary heads about business intelligence, physical security access control, cybersecurity threats, etc.

Mitchell introduced Ferrari to Kastrup, Albert Alioto, and the corporate security director. After several minutes of discussions, he picked up his phone and dialed Ericksen's extension.

"Hello," said Ericksen.

"Mark, we just appointed Tony Ferrari of *AUF Consulting Group* for a six-month contract. I believe you knew him when he was the CIA station chief in Bern. If you have a minute, please drop by my office and say hello."

"Will be there in a couple of minutes."

A few minutes later, Ericksen entered Mitchell's office and shook Ferrari's hand. "Lars Wahlberg told me he enjoyed working with you.

And of course, my wife did too."

"Lars did a good job for the Agency. I'm happy that you and your teammate saved Kate's life."

"We had luck on our side," replied Ericksen.

"Agree. Perhaps later, we can get together for dinner with you and Kate."

"Definitely."

They spent the next several minutes talking and then left Mitchell's office.

Ferrari would start on January 15. He needed to find a motel like the Residence Inn or sublet an apartment that *Cyberburst Communications* might assist him in finding. He now had to begin the planning stages to kill Wahlberg up in Oregon.

Chapter Twenty-One

Over the following two weeks, Ferrari got together with Ericksen and McDonald over lunch and dinner. He was in the process of establishing a friendship with them. Little did they know what devious plans he had in store.

Ferrari emailed Sorokin on February 10, asking for Evgeny to meet him in California. He received his reply several days later, Evgeny would call him when he arrived in California.

Sorokin flew to Miami from Zurich on February 23. He spent several days with his uncle, who had become a naturalized American citizen ten years earlier. His uncle lived in an expensive luxury condominium in Sunny Isles, Florida. One evening he took Sorokin to dinner at an exclusive country club called Mar-a-Lago in Palm Beach. His uncle was a real estate investor, married, with two adult children who lived nearby in Boca Raton. Sorokin had a fabulous time with his uncle, aunt, and cousins. He enjoyed swimming in the large pool and the ocean, hitting the night clubs, and meeting other wealthy Russians who owned expensive condominiums and luxury homes. Sorokin flew out on the morning of the 29th.

At 12:30 pm, Wednesday afternoon, February 29, Ferrari received a call on his cell phone.

"Hi Tony, this is Evgeny. I am staying at the Holiday Inn in Foster City. When are you available to meet me?"

"How about 8:30 tonight?" replied Ferrari.

"Alright, I'll be waiting outside for you. What kind of car are you driving?"

"I'm driving a Black Audi A4 with Virginia plates. I'll flash my headlights when I see you."

At two in the afternoon, a Russian diplomat who worked undercover as a Russian foreign intelligence officer at the Russian consulate in San Francisco gave a trusted naturalized Russian American, an envelope to give to Evgeny at the hotel.

One hour later, Evgeny met the young man in the restroom near the lobby. The note gave instructions to go to Laurelwood Park and hike up the trail, which led to Sugarloaf Mountain. Inside the envelope was a map of the route. The plan detailed where he had buried a backpack and where a specific bench was located.

Evgeny drove his rental car to the park. He followed the trail and reached the spot. Behind the bench were large trees, and ten feet to the right, an empty Perrier water bottle was lying on the ground. He took out his small shovel from his backpack, dug one foot underneath the soft bed of soil, and reached the new treasure. He dropped his gear in the disposal and drove back to the hotel with the new backpack. Once he went to his room, he opened the backpack and saw three cyanide spray guns.

Evgeny spotted Ferrari's black Audi A4. He got into the car, drove to the San Mateo Hilton Garden Inn, and parked the car. He called Sorokin's cell phone. Sorokin heard his phone vibrate and removed it from his rear pocket.

"Hello," he said in Russian.

"Evgeny here. What room are you in?"

"Room 207."

Ferrari and Evgeny entered Sorokin's room and sat on the couch. They began making plans to drive up to Portland and conduct surveillance on Wahlberg. Ferrari provided Sorokin with one cyanide spray gun and three 9mm Makarov .380 caliber ACPs with ammo. He gave them the address of *Cyberburst Biometrics* headquarters in Wilsonville and Wahlberg's home address in Lake Oswego.

"I plan to set up a dinner meeting at a restaurant in either Lake Oswego or Tualatin. You can kill him in the restroom or when he walks to his car in the parking lot."

"We'll be leaving tomorrow morning for Portland," said Sorokin.

WILSONVILLE, OREGON

Ferrari called Wahlberg on March 5 at his Wilsonville office.

"It's Tony. I would like to meet with you and discuss conducting a security audit for your company. Would you be available on Tuesday, March 13?"

"Hold on, let me check my schedule."

Wahlberg pulled out his laptop computer and checked his calendar. "That will work. How many days would you need with my key personnel?"

"Probably two days. Are you open for dinner on Thursday?" asked Ferrari.

"I look forward to it."

"Do you want to meet at the Golden Goose Restaurant on Bangy Road?" asked Ferrari.

"We can't go wrong with the Golden Goose. What time?"

"Can you meet me at seven?" asked Wahlberg.

"Got it. See you soon."

On Thursday, Ferrari secured a table at the restaurant and was waiting for Wahlberg to join him. A few minutes later, he entered the restaurant, and the host escorted him to Ferrari's table. Sorokin and Evgeny were sitting at the bar and had a good view of both men. Sorokin wore an Oregon Ducks baseball hat, large-rim glasses, and a blue oversized North Face jacket with several pockets. Inside one of his pockets hid a small aluminum cylinder spray gun that ejected liquid cyanide.

It was about 9:00 pm when they finished their dinner. Ferrari paid with his credit card, and they got up to leave. "I'm going to the restroom," said Wahlberg.

Ferrari stood against the wall, not far from the place the host was stationed and waited.

Sorokin followed Wahlberg into the restroom and noticed that no one else was in there. Evgeny was loitering near the bathroom to watch if anyone entered. While Wahlberg was urinating in a urinal separated by a metal divider, Sorokin approached from behind, removed his cyanide spray gun, and squeezed the trigger, ejecting the poison gas from a crushed cyanide capsule into Wahlberg's neck. He immediately was in a state of shock as he struggled for a few seconds, unable to speak; the vapors and fluids were racing through his body and paralyzing him. Wahlberg dropped to the floor and died. The poison induced cardiac arrest. Sorokin immediately left the bathroom, followed by Evgeny, and walked out of the restaurant. They jogged a block to where their rental car was parked.

A minute later, a sixty-year-old man entered the restroom, and when he saw the man on the floor, he screamed and ran out to tell the host. The host called the manager, and ten seconds later, he entered the restroom with Ferrari.

Ferrari felt Wahlberg's pulse. "I think he's dead."

The manager took out his cellphone and called the Lake Oswego Police.

Ten minutes later, several police officers arrived with three paramedics from the Tualatin Valley Fire and Rescue. They pronounced Wahlberg dead. The police questioned Ferrari and the sixty-year-old man who had discovered Wahlberg's body. Then they asked questions to the host and the manager. The paramedics put Wahlberg on a stretcher and took him to the local morgue. The next day Ferrari informed Mitchell and several other people at headquarters and *Cyberburst Biometrics* in Wilsonville of the death of Lars Wahlberg.

Over the next day, Ferrari was questioned further at the police department. The host was the only one who remembered seeing a man wearing an Oregon Ducks baseball hat and glasses entering the restroom after Wahlberg.

Ericksen and his wife flew up to Portland three days later for the funeral, and did their best to comfort Wahlberg's wife. Ericksen called and informed Sullivan. He realized that whoever killed Wahlberg might be inclined to kill them next. He assumed the FBI surveillance of Wahlberg was limited to outside of the restaurant.

On Wednesday, April 4, Kastrup appointed Ericksen senior vice-president of marketing at *Cyberburst Communications*. Ericksen immediately appointed Jeb Templeton to senior vice-president/ general manager of *Cyberburst Biometrics*. Ericksen had confidence Templeton would perform well in his new role.

Chapter Twenty-Two

Thanks to Ericksen's leadership efforts, *Cyberburst Communication* acquired two biometrics technology companies: *Laguna Facial Systems* in San Diego, California, and *Quest Omega Systems*, a fingerprint technology company in Austin, Texas. Kastrup and the board of directors acknowledged that his management approach delivered successful results. Recently one of his teams had successfully secured orders for satellite warfare software with a principal defense contractor. Ericksen, along with his division marketing managers and their teams submitted several tenders for potential orders from the aerospace and defense establishment and the intelligence community.

MOSCOW

On April 10, 2012, Sorokin appointed Dimitri, a thirty-eight-year-old, dark-haired former captain of the Russian GRU to his assassination team. Dimitri worked for Colonel Oleg Kupchenko years earlier. Now he represented Ryzhkov's mining companies and traveled to the United States twice a year. He was tall, lean, and muscular. His other known work for Ryzhkov was as a hitman. He was commissioned with Ryzhkov's approval to do hits for Moscow's organized crime family.

PALO ALTO

Kastrup held a meeting on April 18 in his office with Mitchell, Ericksen, Ferrari, their corporate security director, and the CFO. They talked about the death of Wahlberg up in Portland.

After the meeting, Kastrup met with Feldman and played racketball at the Palo Alto Esquire Club. While in the steam room, he turned to Kastrup and asked, "Have you thought about my offer to buy your shares of the company?"

"Sid, I'm not interested in selling my shares to your company yet. Before I am ready to retire and sell the company, I want to groom my company's replacement. If my instincts are on target, it will be Mark Ericksen."

"Ericksen! What about Logan Mitchell?"

"Mitchell is a good man, but I'm looking for a visionary with top leadership qualities. Ericksen fits the bill perfectly. He has all the attributes of growing *Cyberburst Communications* to new heights, and he knows team building."

The next morning, Feldman met with Mitchell for coffee at Feldman Capital Group's office. He informed Mitchell about his conversation with Kastrup, and Mitchell was in shock. The news hit him like a tsunami.

"After serving as COO of the company, you would think I would be the ideal successor," Mitchell said. After his retirement in 2006 as a major general working for the Defense Department, he joined the company. He stood 5'10", was lean and muscular, and weighed about 160 pounds.

Over the next several evenings, one could find Mitchell at the Rosewood Sand Hill Hotel drinking with friends. One evening, he scheduled a meeting with Ferrari to discuss the security issues of several subsidiaries. After downing three glasses of Remy Martin XO cognac, he looked straight into Ferrari's eyes. "According to reliable sources, Ericksen is being groomed as Kastrup's replacement when he steps down."

"No way! I can't understand how Kastrup could pass you up for Ericksen."

At that moment, Ferrari thought of making a profitable deal by killing Kastrup and making Mitchell the new CEO.

On Monday, April 23, Ferrari, Ericksen, and Mitchell were having dinner at Riccardo's Italian Restaurant in the Stanford Shopping Center.

Over the next hour of heavy drinking, Mitchell got drunk, and Ferrari offered to drive him home. Ferrari went to the restroom, sat on the toilet in the stall, and texted Evgeny to get to the parking lot. He and Dimitri were seated at the bar when the text appeared on Evengy's cell phone.

Ferrari escorted Mitchell to the parking lot. He walked him to his car, opened the passenger door, and gently helped him into the passenger seat. Ferrari lowered the window and waved to Ericksen, "See you in the morning. Good night."

Ericksen walked toward his new black Rubicon jeep, which was behind a Toyota Highlander SUV. From his peripheral vision, he saw a man walking toward him sixty feet from his right and by a row of cars in the parking lot. He heard footsteps behind him, turned, and saw a man take out something.

Evengy had taken out his cyanide poison spray gun and was now about twenty feet from his target. Ericksen immediately pulled out his Beretta 9mm handgun and fired two shots to the assailant's head. Evgeny dropped to the pavement, blood flowing out of his body, and died.

At that moment, Dimitri fired two shots from his Makarov handgun at Ericksen and missed, then he ducked below the Toyota Highlander. Ericksen's FBI security officer glanced at Dimitri, who stood about thirty feet away from him, and shot him in the head, dropping the Russian to the pavement.

Several people fled the restaurant when they heard gunshots. The restaurant manager and other people took out their cell phones and dialed 911. Ten minutes later, several Palo Alto police cars arrived on the scene. They started asking questions of Ericksen, and he told them those men were trying to kill him. A bystander confirmed to police what he said. At that moment, the FBI security officer produced his credentials to the officers and stated what he saw and that he killed the other man who was attempting to kill Ericksen.

The police asked Ericksen and the FBI security officer to come to the police station and make a statement. Ten minutes later, the police van arrived and placed the dead men in body bags.

Chapter Twenty-Three

LONDON

On April 24, Roger Hanley of MI5, inspector supervisor from the Metropolitan Police, cybersecurity experts from MI6, and GCHQ met with the MI5 director at the Thames House in London.

Hanley began his Powerpoint presentation. "We checked communications from Alexander Ryzhkov's Swiss mobile phone number and the following mobile phone numbers he contacted besides Kublanov." Hanley took a moment to look directly at the MI5 director. "Sir, based on all these calls we retrieved, we recommend scheduling a meeting with the FBI and CIA in Washington D.C. immediately. The CIA may have a mole within their organization."

"I'll review this with the home secretary, MI6. and get back to you."

MOSCOW

On April 25, Ferrari sent an encrypted email to Sorokin about Evengy and Dimitri's deaths in California. Sorokin went to work, took the elevator to the fiftieth floor, and entered the *Ryzhkov Energy and Mining Company* office.

He knocked on Ryzhkov's door and entered.

"I have bad news to report," Sorokin said in Russian. "Evgeny and Dimitri are dead."

"What! What went wrong?" said Ryzhkov, his voice rising.

"Ferrari said Ericksen killed them last night in Palo Alto."

"Damn it! Now how the hell am I going to tell President Gorshkov we messed up. He is going to be furious with us! I want you to set up a meeting with Ferrari immediately. I need you to kill Ericksen and his wife."

"Yes, sir."

The next morning Sorokin sent Ferrari an encrypted email requesting a meeting in San Francisco as soon as possible.

STANFORD SHOPPING CENTER

Ferrari and Mitchell met at Riccardo's Restaurant on Thursday evening, April 26, and sat in the bar drinking. Ever since Mitchell heard about Kastrup's plans, he has been drinking heavily. He was glassy-eyed and slurring his words. He placed his right hand on Ferrari's left wrist. "How many people have you killed?"

"We've all killed our enemies in war," replied Ferrari.

"No, I mean, have you ever killed a foreign spy, or any person not associated with combat?"

"I can't discuss my intelligence service with anyone. I'm sure you understand."

"I want you to promise me what I say to you will be strictly confidential, Mitchell said. "Can I count on you?"

"Of course."

"If Kastrup dies, I believe I would become president and CEO of the company. In a crisis like that, I'm sure the board of directors would appoint me."

"Are you throwing out a suggestion you want Kastrup killed?" asked Ferrari.

"Yes."

"Are you asking me if I would be interested in killing him?" "Affirmative." said Mitchell and looked around the bar and back at Ferrari.

"I'll give you $200 thousand dollars if you agree to the job."

"Let me think about it, and I'll get back to you soon with my answer."

CIA HEADQUARTERS

Roger Hanley, the MI 5 director, and an MI6 officer arrived at the CIA Headquarters in Langley, Virginia, on May 4.

The men were escorted to the seventh floor elevator by two security officers. The CIA director, the Deputy Director of the Clandestine Services, Ken Washington, the FBI director, and Defense Secretary Sullivan were all sitting in the SCIF conference room next to the CIA director's office. The CIA director turned to Sullivan and the others.

"Mr. Hanley has information regarding former General Alexander Ryzhkov and his potential involvement in the killing of Igor Kublanov."

Hanley stood up and began his Powerpoint presentation:

"Ryzhkov called Berlin number 49-30-41960 from Swiss mobile phone number 41-41-5536428 on July 4, and according to the mobile phone towers, both people were in Moscow."

"He called Kublanov from his Swiss number in London on July 12, 2011."

"We also checked back to the beginning of 2011."

"The Berlin number called from London to an *AUF Consulting Group's* mobile phone number on 3/21/2011. However, the receiver was in Paris. The owner of that mobile phone number is Anthony Ferrari."

"A Cambridge burner mobile phone number called the Berlin mobile phone number on March 21, 2011, from London. Both men who had possession of their respective mobile phones were physically in London at the time."

"From London, the individual who had the Berlin mobile phone sent a text message to Ryzhkov's Swiss mobile phone on March 21, 2011, who picked it up in Moscow."

"Ryzhkov called a burner phone number with a Cambridge

number on September 2, 2011: from the Holiday Inn Crown Express, Hounslow, from his Swiss mobile phone number. Both men who had possession of those mobile phones were physically at the Holiday Inn Crown Express."

"Ryzhkov received a call on his Swiss mobile phone number from a mobile phone registered to a McLean, Virginia address on December 7, 2010. Both parties were in Monte Carlo, Monaco. Again, it was from Anthony Ferrari."

"Ken Washington, the CIA's station chief at the U.S. Embassy in London, using the alias Bob Richmond, received a call on his encrypted mobile phone from *AUF Consulting Group's* mobile phone on March 21, 2011. The caller was Anthony Ferrari, who called from Paris."

"Washington received a call on his cell phone from a burner phone later with a Cambridge number. Both parties were in London."

"The persons we are most interested in are Alexander Ryzhkov and Viktor Sorokin. Both men were in London on July 12 and were registered at the Sheraton Hotel in Knightsbridge from July 12 through 14. We know from our interviews with Kublanov's wife that they were invited for dinner at their home on the evening of the 14th. We believe they planned to kill Kublanov because he supported Gorshkov's rival in the upcoming presidential elections. However, we also found out from both Sorokin's Berlin mobile phone number and Ryzhkov's Swiss mobile phone number they have been communicating with one of your former CIA operators, Anthony Ferrari."

"When did that occur?" asked the CIA director.

Sullivan moved forward in his chair. Washington's eyes opened wide, and he glanced at the CIA director.

"Sorokin was in London on 3/21/2011, when he called Ferrari's mobile phone. Ferrari answered the call from Paris. Ryzhkov received a call from Ferrari's mobile phone on December 7, 2010, and both were in Monte Carlo."

"Mr. Washington, what was discussed with you and Ferrari on his call to you on March 21?" asked Hanley.

Everyone stared at Washington.

"Tony wanted to get together with me for dinner that night," said Washington.

"What was discussed during your dinner?"

Washington, puzzled by the question, looked around the room before answering.

"We talked about family, his new consulting job, and Russian intelligence agencies assassinating Russian businessmen over the past several years in Britain."

Sullivan looked straight at Washington. "Was there anything peculiar or surprising about Ferrari's demeanor or questions?"

"He asked me if we heard anything from our sources about a threat to Igor Kublanov's life since he supported Gorshkov's rival," replied Washington.

Sullivan pressed on. "Was there anything else you thought strange or out of place during Ferrari's meeting with you?"

Washington looked up, shook his head a few times, then placed his hands firmly on the table. "Ferrari called me when he arrived in London, but this time he was using a burner phone. I asked him if this was a burner phone, and he confirmed it. In our line of work, it was not unusual, but I wondered why he would call me on it."

The FBI director asked Washington, "Do you happen to have that number?"

"Yes." Washington said, and took out his notebook from his briefcase. "The burner mobile number was 01223-439639."

"We know for sure Ferrari used his burner phone on March 21, 2011, to call Washington. He also contacted the Berlin mobile phone number that same day, and both he and the party were communicating from London. He also was in contact with Ryzhkov on September 2, and they were both calling each other from the same hotel in Hounslow, England," Hanley said.

"Ferrari needs to be under FBI counterintelligence surveillance immediately," Sullivan said.

The FBI director nodded his head in agreement. "I'll submit a warrant to authorize wiretapping to the judge for Ferrari's condominium, and I'll assign one of our best counterintelligence agents."

Chapter Twenty-Four

SAN FRANCISCO BAY AREA

Defense Secretary Sullivan and his security detail arrived on a Gulfstream G650 Jet on Saturday, May 5, at NASA Ames Research Center, Moffett Field, in Mountain View, California. The security detail drove him to Ericksen's home in Menlo Park.

After being warmly greeted by McDonald and Ericksen, they assembled in the living room. McDonald's mother from Sandpoint, Idaho, had arrived the day before to help with the baby. Over the next fifteen minutes, they discussed family matters and the joy their six-month-old baby girl has brought them.

"Do you you time for dinner?" asked Ericksen.

"Thanks, but I'm having dinner at my daughter's place in Mill Valley tonight, and spending a few days with her family before flying back to Washington."

"In my duffel bag is our updated version of the Hummingbird robot drone and laser ear microphone. It's equipped with a high-end video camera and zoom lens and can transmit images back to your vehicle from up to two hundred yards away."

Ericksen reflected for a moment, *Operation Avenging Eagles* used the original Hummingbird robot drone successfully in gathering intelligence from the Saudi mastermind's headquarters in Jeddah two years earlier.

"Any more news about Sorokin's arrival here?" asked Ericksen. "NSA picked up a call from Sorokin's Berlin cell phone to a burner phone in San Mateo about arriving on Lufthansa on Tuesday, May 8. He used his German alias, Gerhard Richter, and is booked at the Hyatt Regency by the airport."

Sorokin flew into San Francisco International Airport on Tuesday evening, May 8. He called Ferrari to meet him in his hotel room at the Hyatt Regency San Francisco Airport Hotel on Wednesday at 4:00 in the afternoon on May 9.

Sullivan sent an encrypted email to Ericksen, providing him with Ferrari's new burner phone number with a San Mateo County area code.

Ericksen had a female FBI counterintelligence officer watching in the hotel's lobby when Sorokin registered. She waited until Sorokin approached the elevator and entered with him. He pressed the sixth floor. When the elevator door opened, he went to the left, and she dropped an envelope, giving her a chance to watch the room number he entered. He entered room number 620. She turned around and pressed the elevator button to go back to the lobby. Once she sat down on one of the lobby chairs, she called Ericksen with the room number.

At 4:10 pm, Ferrari entered Sorokin's room and walked toward the couch in the suite. Sorokin opened the minibar, "Wolfgang, what would you like to drink?"

"How about a beer?"

Sorokin reached into the mini-bar and pulled out two beers.

The Hummingbird drone maintained a level pattern directly outside Sorokin's room. The laser ear microphone transmitted an infra-red beam to the window, generating vibrations into a modulated sound converted into electronic signals by the receiver in Ericksen's black Rubicon jeep, and started recording.

After a few minutes of conversation, Sorokin said, "Your advance of $1 million covered Wahlberg's hit. When I received your email last week informing me Ericksen would not be in town during my stay, I advised Ryzhkov. After we kill McDonald, you'll receive a final payment of 1 million dollars wired to your private numbered bank account."

Ferrari's facial expression went blank. "What do you mean final payment? We still have until the first week of September to kill Ericksen" said Ferrari, raising his voice.

"Your agreement on Ericksen has been canceled!"

"Ryzhkov promised me I had till September 2 of this year to fulfill the agreement," said Ferrari.

"President Gorshkov was pissed off after he heard Evengy and Dimitri were killed, and he overruled Ryzhkov," said Sorokin.

Ferrari regained his composure, and recognized the decision was final. He took a swig of beer and said, "I need a favor from you. I want your cybersecurity people to gain control of an important individual's 2011 Mercedes in Palo Alto and activate the accelerator to shoot up to 100 miles an hour on a certain date and time in the immediate future."

"That can be done. However, we will need the make and model of the Mercedes, the VIN, the license plate number, the identity of the owner of the vehicle, and where the individual services his car," said Sorokin.

"I will take care of it for you."

"Thanks." said Ferrari and continued, "How would you like to join me for dinner at Benihana's japanese steakhouse?"

"That's a good idea," replied Sorokin.

Ferrari stood up and picked up his briefcase and they left the room. They got into Ferrari's rental car and drove a few blocks to 1496 Old Bayshore Highway, in Burlingame. When they entered the restaurant the hostess escorted them to the bar. They both ordered a Japanese beer.

"Perhaps you can get an opportunity to terminate Ericksen when he is in Europe because he will be conducting a European sales distributors' conference on September 3-5 along with Jeb Templeton, his senior vice-president and general manager of *Cyberburst Biometrics.*"

"Where is it being held?"

"The conference will be held at the Persson Resort in the town of Klintehamn, on the Swedish Island of Gotland," said Ferrari, as he opened up his briefcase and handed the information about the conference to Sorokin.

"Good. Ryzhkov will be happy to hear the news."

"Kate McDonald meets a friend for breakfast at a restaurant every Friday in Woodside," Ferrari said, 'and then they go for a three-mile hike in a heavily forested area in Wunderlich County Park. I will call her up tomorrow morning and see if I can join them for breakfast. Hopefully, she'll allow me to join her for a hike on Friday."

"Let's get in touch tomorrow morning at 7:30 and plan on meeting at 10:00 at Wunderlich County Park and check out the trails," said Sorokin.

Later that night, Sorokin emailed Ryzhkov the details of the upcoming conference.

LOS ALTOS HILLS

The FBI received the approval on their warrant to wiretap Logan Mitchell's home on Morningside Circle in Los Altos Hills. On Wednesday evening, Ferrari and Mitchell sat in the study and discussed the plan to kill Kastrup. The FBI team used the Hummingbird drone to listen in.

Ferrari poured a shot of vodka and downed it with one gulp.

"Our hackers will be ready to take control of Kastrup's Mercedes soon. We will plan it for a particular time when he leaves his office to go home. Once you send me an email with a code several hours in advance of the targeted time, my people will be on standby and activate the plan with the precise time."

"Good." said Mitchell, "You drive a hard bargain. I'm glad you decided to accept my final offer of $500,000 for the hit on Kastrup."

"I need you to wire $250,000 to my bank in Switzerland tomorrow. The balance upon Kastrup's death."

"Confirmed."

Ferrari took out a sheet of paper with the numbered account at Monch and Schneider Private Bank's office on Bahnhofstrasse in Zurich and handed it to Mitchell. "Here are the instructions for the wire transfer to the Monch and Schneider Bank in Zurich."

Mitchell nodded, stood up, and shook Ferrari's hand.

Two FBI agents gathered all their equipment and drove away in their van with the damaging evidence against Ferrari and Mitchell.

WOODSIDE, CALIFORNIA

Jeb Templeton arrived Wednesday evening from Portland. He rented a car and drove to his in-laws in Portola Valley for a two-night stay.

He picked up Ericksen at 7:45 am on Thursday and drove to Alice's Restaurant on Skyline Boulevard in Woodside. They arrived two minutes after it opened, and Ericksen ordered a coffee with the special: Alice's three-egg omelet with avocado, applewood smoked bacon, swiss cheese, and tomato. Templeton ordered scrambled eggs with hash browns, whole-wheat toast, and coffee with cream.

At 9:30 am, Ericksen began his hike from Alice's Restaurant, up Skyline Trail, and Alambique Trail to Bear Gulch Trail, and stopped at the Meadow Trail. Wunderlich County Park consisted of beautiful canyons and many springs through almost a thousand acres of mixed forest and meadowland. Ericksen smelled the sweet fresh park's air and was in awe of the abundance of redwood, oak, California laurel, douglas fir, and madrone trees.

The FBI counterintelligence team placed surveillance on Ferrari and Sorokin, who had just arrived at Alice's Restaurant parking area. They alerted Ericksen as the two men began hiking up the Skyline Trail. The team on the ground coordinated with a drone overhead. They watched Ferrari and Sorokin take the Alambique trail and noted where Sorokin would probably attack McDonald when she appeared. The spot for the ambush was approximately one mile from Alice's Restaurant. Based on the FBI team's drone view, they provided Ericksen a location with lots of brush and redwood trees.

When Ferrari had called McDonald, she agreed to meet him at

Alice's Restaurant on Friday morning at 8:00. Her husband had already briefed her on the plan. It was a dangerous request, but she trusted him, and they needed to take aggressive action to finish the threats to their lives.

On Friday morning, she met Ferrari at Alice's Restaurant. They managed to find an outside table under an umbrella with a view of the forest.

"Where is your friend?" asked Ferrari.

"She fell sick and canceled."

They both ordered Alice's special, and Earl Grey tea.

Templeton watched them from his car and noticed Ferrari pointing to the parking lot and Kate looking away. In the few seconds of distraction, he poured something into her tea.

Templeton immediately called her cell phone. "Kate, it's Jeb. Act relaxed, but I saw Ferrari pour something in your tea."

"Thanks, I'll call her tomorrow, and we can plan to take our babies out to the park," said Kate.

The waiter delivered their order. Then Kate knocked the cup of tea off the table.

"Sorry. I'm so clumsy."

"Can we have another cup, please?" asked Ferrari.

"On second thought, I want a bold cup of coffee," said Kate. Twenty minutes later, they left the restaurant and hiked up the Skyline Trail.

Ericksen began hiking down the Bear Gulch Trail toward the targeted spot for the ambush. He heard several pecks above the trees. He looked up and saw a woodpecker chipping away. There were all types of birds and wild animals in the park: deer, coyotes, foxes, bobcats, and occasionally, cougars.

The FBI drone located Sorokin on the Alambique Trail near the Skyline Trail. Ericksen removed his Beretta handgun and placed a suppressor on it. He gripped the firearm with his right hand.

Ferrari and McDonald were 900 feet from Sorokin and hiking at a good pace. Ericksen moved slowly and closer to the target. He spotted Sorokin near a tall Redwood tree surrounded by lots of brush.

He closed in on his target and stopped when he was sixty feet from him. He now held his handgun firmly in his hands. Suddenly he made his move twenty feet from his target, aiming his gun right at Sorokin's head.

Ericksen called out, "Viktor Sorokin, drop the cyanide spray gun, or I'll fire!"

Sorokin's eyes shot up; his face tightened by the surprising sound of the male voice. When he did not drop the spray gun, Ericksen moved within ten feet of Sorokin and raised his voice. "You son-of-a-bitch, you killed my friend Lars Wahlberg."

Sorokin glanced at Ericksen and raised the cyanide poison spray gun when Ericksen shot it out of his hand. The next two shots from his gun hit Sorokin in his right shoulder and left knee. Sorokin immediately fell to the ground and yelled in Russian, "You rotten bastard!"

Ericksen picked up the poison cyanide spray gun and, standing three feet from Sorokin, aimed the spray gun at him and spoke firmly, "Now, you low-life parasite, rot in hell!"

He squeezed the trigger, and the poison hit Sorokin in the neck. He went into shock and shook all over as the poison fluid rushed through his body, paralyzing him, and died.

Ferrari and Kate were within 120 feet from where Sorokin's body was lying on the forest ground. Templeton was 60 feet behind them. Suddenly, Ferrari saw Ericksen appear from behind the douglas fir trees with his handgun aimed at Ferrari's head. Kate moved behind her husband, and Templeton arrived with his gun pointed at him too.

"Behind the redwood tree, roughly 100 feet away is Sorokin's body."

Ericksen turned to his wife, handed her the Beretta, and said, "Please do us the honor of killing this fucking traitor."

Surprised by her husband's words, she firmly gripped the handgun, walked within ten feet of Ferrari, and said, "You put all of our lives in danger, and now it's your time to die."

She squeezed the trigger hitting Ferrari in the forehead. He fell to the ground and died. This was the second time McDonald had killed a person. Two years earlier, she killed Oleg Kupchenko, the Russian arms dealer who abducted and sexually assaulted her.

Ten minutes later, the FBI counterterrorism task force brought body bags and scooped up Sorokin and Ferrari. They drove the bodies to the San Mateo County Morgue.

The next day, the Russian consulate and the Russian embassy received word of the death of Sorokin. The State Department informed the Russian government to pick up his body. Their answer came back the next day. "We don't know this person. Therefore, you can do whatever you wish."

The FBI had a more sensitive issue regarding Ferrari's body. In the next few days, they would contact Ferrari's ex-wife, brother, and adult children and notify them of his death. Arrangements had been made to ship his body to Virginia. Details of his death would be treated with sensitivity and confidentiality.

Chapter Twenty-Five

PALO ALTO

"He was a secret agent and still alive thanks to his exact attention to the detail of his profession."
Ian Fleming

On Monday, May 14, the Los Altos police arrested Mitchell on solicitation charges and conspiracy to commit homicide. He posted bail and was released several hours later. The FBI informed Kastrup that they had collected evidence from their investigation proving Mitchell and Ferrari had planned to kill him.

CIA HEADQUARTERS

The CIA collected actionable intelligence from hacking Ryzhkov's and Schroeder's encrypted cell phones. The men planned a meeting at the Chateau Rosenberg in Gstaad, Switzerland, July 11-13. Their findings also implicated the Iranian intelligence director Esmail Beheshti and Reza Nabavi, the Iranian Revolutionary Guard Commander. Their meeting involved more intensive support for President Bashar al-

Assad of Syria and solidifying the Mediterranean Sea's Russian naval facility. Those discussions were finalized on June 13 in Moscow when Ryzhkov and his lieutenants were having lunch with Schroeder at Café Pushkin.

PALO ALTO

On Thursday, June 7, Ericksen finished a meeting with Poul Kastrup and the CFO and returned to his office. They decided to keep the position of COO of the company vacant for several months. However, Kastrup announced the following day the appointment of Mark Ericksen as executive vice-president. The announcement was released to the press. Further discussions would be on the agenda for the board of directors meeting at the end of September.

Ericksen's encrypted cell phone rang. On the second ring, he picked it up.

"Sullivan here. I have good news for you. Alexander Ryzhkov is planning to meet Reza Nabavi and Heinrich Schroeder at the Chateau Rosenberg in Gstaad, Switzerland, July 11-13. Are you interested in finishing the job?"

"Damn right, sir!" said a jubilant Ericksen.

"I'll be in contact with the director-general of Mossad. I'm sure he might have someone interested in being in Gstaad at the same time."

"If anything goes wrong, we will disavow any involvement in this matter," said Sullivan.

"I'll make plans immediately."

Ericksen needed additional support for this executive action and contacted his Norwegian distributor, Thomas Andersen, a former special forces member of his platoon during *Operation Enduring Freedom* in Afghanistan.

Sullivan contacted his former CIA chief-of-staff, who was now retired. He told him to call a vacation rental agency in Gstaad immediately and make reservations for a four bedroom, three bath chalet from Monday, July 9, through Monday, July 16. His last statement to him was, "My two boys will arrive on Monday evening."

MOSCOW

On Tuesday, June 12, Ryzhkov called from his secured landline to President Gorshkov's direct encrypted telephone at the palatial residence outside Moscow. "Misha, are you interested in joining me for the Siberian brown bear hunt near Lake Baikal August 22 through August 28?"

"We haven't been on a brown bear hunt in years. Let me think about it and get back to you next week. On another topic, sorry to hear about Sorokin's death. We need to get rid of Ericksen."

"I agree."

"You recently mentioned that Ericksen will be conducting a sales conference on Gotland Island for three days starting September 5. One of my most trusted executives is Igor Turgenev. Since becoming deputy director of the FSB, he has done an excellent job for me."

"He has assisted me on several occasions when he was the station chief of the SVR in Switzerland," said Ryzhkov.

"Sasha, I will have Turgenev set up a meeting with you, and I want you to provide him the file on Ericksen."

"Can you be available to meet with him on Friday morning?"

"How is 10 o'clock?"

"Sounds good."

On Wednesday, June 13, Ryzhkov took his executive assistant to lunch at the Café Pushkin on Tverskoi Boulevard by Pushkin Square. The CIA operative who began conducting surveillance on Ryzhkov knew he had lunch every Wednesday at Café Pushkin around 1:00 pm whenever he was in town. Ryzhkov sat at his reserved table while the operative was seated at the following table with an undercover British Embassy female who worked as a diplomat for MI6.

Ryzhkov looked directly at his executive assistant. "I want you to meet our important guest when he arrives around 10:00 am this Friday at the express elevator," said Ryzhkov.

"I'll be there, sir!"

That evening, the CIA operative passed the information up the chain to Langley. The CIA director tasked the Moscow station chief to direct an operative to be in the lobby on Friday at 10:00 am, near the express elevator.

RYZHKOV ENERGY AND MINING COMPANY

On Friday, June 15, Ryzhkov's executive assistant met Igor Turgenev at 10:00 am in the Moscow International Business Center lobby. Turgenev dressed in a dark blue suit, white shirt, and red and blue tie. His wavy brown hair, large broken nose, and the scars along his left cheek and above his right eyebrow were quite noticeable. If looks could kill, Turgenev had a lock on it. The forty-five-year-old spy had a reputation for killing opponents of the Russian Federation and Russian spies who changed their allegiance from loyalty to the Kremlin.

The CIA operative scrolled the business directory for a few minutes, turned to see an attractive woman standing next to the elevator and talking to a man he immediately knew as Igor Turgenev, the deputy director of the Russian domestic intelligence agency, FSB. The operative dressed in a simple gray business suit, white shirt, and black tie, took out his ballpoint pen and a small pad of paper to write one of the businesses on the directory. Then turned toward Turgenev and pressed the ballpoint pen which housed a camouflaged miniature camera to take the picture, and then placed the pen back inside his suit pocket.

The executive assistant and the master spy took the elevator to the 50th floor and entered the lobby. A few minutes later, Turgenev met Ryzhkov and spent the next two hours discussing the abduction of Mark Ericksen and killing Jeb Templeton.

"Igor Yurievich, you are Russia's best assassin, but you must be on your top game against Ericksen."

"Don't worry about me. My team will abduct him and deliver him to President Gorshkov."

"The president wants to personally torture and kill him when you bring him to Lubyanka headquarters, said Ryzhkov smiling, and continuing, "Are you up for a couple of handball games?"

"General, I was hoping you would ask me. Just don't get upset if I beat your ass."

MOSCOW, PRESIDENT GORSHKOV'S RESIDENCE

On June 22, A bullet-proof Mercedes SUV drove up to the President's driveway, escorted by two armored Mercedes SUVs. Turgenev got out of the SUV and was ushered into the palatial residence by two body-guards. They directed him to the office of Gorshkov's chief-of- staff. A few minutes later, Turgenev was directed into the office.

They both greeted each other with hugs and kissed on each cheek. Turgenev followed in Gorshkov's footsteps. He graduated from Moscow State University, became a special forces officer in Spetsnaz, and after several years of service, was recruited by the SVR. His language skills were excellent. He spoke German, French and English. He also attained a 4th degree belt in Judo, and black belts in Takwondo, and Samba. His skill as a national champion in handball was especially appreciated by Gorshkov, who played matches with him from time to time.

"Let's discuss the planning of the operation. Tell me the elements of the plan, Igor Yuryevich" Gorshkov said.

"First of all, Heinrich and Otto Schroeder own property on the east side of Gotland Island. I will fly to Stockholm from Kyiv around Tuesday, August 28, on forged Ukrainian passports. One of my senior FSB operators will be on the same flight. Otto will pick us up at the Visby airport, and he will drive us to his summer home.

Kirill and two of his FSB agents from the Operational Reconnaissance Directorate will arrive on Wednesday, August 29, and will be on a flight from Frankfurt to Stockholm to Visby with forged Swiss passports. Otto will have someone pick them up at the airport.

Secondly, the Schroeders' have weapons, bulletproof vests, disguises, and other support gear for our eventual abduction of Ericksen. We're assuming he will be traveling back to the Visby airport with Jeb Templeton, his general manager of Cyberburst Biometrics. We plan to kill Templeton and tranqualize Ericksen.

Thirdly, we'll go over the routes Ericksen and Templeton will take to the airport, make necessary arrangements to hijack vans, trucks or vehicles in the incursion, and plan to evade any police or others who wish to follow us. We'll get rid of the vehicles several miles later and use Schroeder's van for the drive to his mansion.

We will lay low for a day or two, and then Schroeder will have his mega yacht ready for leaving the harbor with all of us on board. Once we are on board we will secure Ericksen in a cabin, his hands flex-cuffed and tied to a chair. We'll have a guard outside the cabin door."

"What about the crew members and the captain of their boat? asked Gorshkov.

"Otto Schroeder told me they were formerly in the German Navy and are part of a criminal gang out of Hamburg. They will keep everything confidential. If not, we will terminate them," said Turgenev.

"Igor, once you advise the GRU of the time of your departure from the marina, our best frigate will depart the port of St. Petersburg for the rendezvous," said Gorshkov.

GSTAAD, SWITZERLAND

On July 9, Ericksen rented a BMW X-5 SUV series at Frankfurt International Airport. An hour later, he picked up the Israeli team, consisting of Yossi Roubini and a dark-haired, olive-skinned attractive woman in her late thirties. The Israelis flew in on forged passports. Their destination was Gstaad. On the way, they stopped off at a CIA safe house on the outskirts of Munich and picked up two CIA cyanide dart guns, assault rifles, handguns, tools, bulletproof vests, and accessories.

Around 10:30 pm, they arrived at a chalet along the river Saane, on Gschwendstrasse in Saanen, about one mile from Gstaad. They were met by Sullivan's trusted American friend, who welcomed the men and woman with some fine Swiss beers.

Roubini received advanced intel from the Office that Schroeder's favorite place to hike was along Lake Lauenen. On Tuesday, Ericksen joined Roubini and the female Mossad assassin for a hike along Lake

Lauenen. They were conducting reconnaissance of several places most viable for killing the men.

That evening they stopped for dinner at Restaurant Sonnenhof in Saanen. Their main entrée was Rahmschnitzel and some Swiss beers.

When they got back to the chalet, they opened a Stags Leap Cabernet Sauvignon wine from California. Roubini lifted his glass of wine and proposed a toast: "To your health. May our mission be successful."

Ericksen lifted his wine glass and clicked Roubini's and the Israeli woman's glass for a toast, and said, "Mazel tov."

"I've heard Schroeder enjoys hiking. Hopefully, he will persuade Nabavi to join him."

"Let us hope, my friend," said Ericksen.

CHATEAU ROSENBERG

On Wednesday, July 11, Alexander Ryzhkov and his wife registered for a tower suite. Ericksen's Norwegian friend and Scandinavian distributor Thomas Andersen and his wife Ragnhild, arrived and checked in at the hotel registration desk.

When the bellman brought their luggage to their room, Ragnhild asked "Do you know what room our friend Mr. Ryzhkov is in?"

He looked at her and said, 'I'm sorry. It is hotel policy not to disclose the registered guests' rooms."

"I understand." She gave him a fifty euro note.

"Thank you very much," he said, and looked into her eyes and said, "Please don't mention this to anyone, but Mr. Ryzhkov is in the top tower suite overlooking the swimming pool. Room number 501."

To verify Ryzhkov's room number, Israel's unit 8200 and the NSA hacked into the Chateau Rosenberg's main computer. Minutes later, the information came back: "Affirmative."

Heinrich Schroeder and his security guard checked in at 4:00 pm. Reza Nabavi and his two security guards checked in at 4:30 pm. Iran's ministry of intelligence got sick and could not make the trip.

Ericksen received intel from the CIA that Ryzhkov enjoyed taking a sauna between five and six whenever he stayed in luxury hotels on business. If the information was correct, he planned to take a sauna using Andersen's guest key the next day.

Later that evening, Ericksen and Roubini found out through unit 8200, Nabavi and Schroeder's room numbers were assigned. They set up the Hummingbird and began listening to their communications. Schroeder and Nabavi spoke about going to Lauenen tomorrow after-noon and hike the 3.2 kilometer loop hike around the lake, called Lauenensee.

LAUENEN, SWITZERLAND

Heinrich Schroeder, Reza Nabavi, and their two bodyguards left at 1:30 pm for a short drive to Lauenen, a picturesque village near Gstaad. Once they reached the parking area, they began their 3.2 kilo-meter loop hike of the Lauenensee.

The Israeli assassins were already set up and in place within the heavily forested hiking paths connecting several rapids and waterfalls along the way to the lake.

Roubini and the female operative carried Heckler & Koch G36 assault rifles, along with the 5.56 x 45mm NATO cartridges and 30-round detachable box magazines. The Mossad assassin set up behind several large rocks and brush. Roubini was forty yards forward and lying prone behind a large pine tree.

The Israeli assassins spotted the four men as they were rounding a bend on the heavily forested hiking trail. They were sixty yards away. The female assassin immediately fired her assault rifle, killing the two bodyguards. Then Roubini stood up and ran toward Schroeder and Nabavi, who were twenty-five yards from him. He managed to get behind another tree, take aim, and cut Schroeder down with three shots. Nabavi turned, lifted his Israeli Baby Eagle handgun from his waist, then ran for some brush coverage. Roubini stealthily moved like a leopard closing in on its prey. Nabavi stood up, looked around, and decided to make a run for the open field when Roubini placed two shots into his thigh and shoulder, and he fell to the ground.

Roubini rushed to stand over Nabavi, who was writhing in pain and covered with blood. He lifted his handgun, aimed it at Nabavi's forehead, and said in Persian, "This is for my dear friend Hamid Aghajani" and he continued in Hebrew "You filthy swine!"

The bullet ripped through Nabavi's forehead making a large hole, as blood speedily poured out.

The Israelis' packed their weapons in two backpacks and walked rapidly to their rental car.

CHATEAU ROSENBERG

On Thursday, July 12, Ryzhkov was sitting nude on the sauna's top wooden bench. Ericksen dyed his hair black, wore large-framed glasses, adjusted a beard over his face, and took the elevator to Andersen's room. The time was 5:00 pm. The NSA and Israel's unit 8200 manipulated the hotel's computer causing it to still-frame and freeze the video cameras on the fifth floor, the elevator video camera, and the video camera at the spa entrance.

Ericksen put on a robe and placed his clothes and shoes into a large laundry bag. Andersen and his wife were also wearing robes. They walked down the corridor to the elevator and pressed the button for the 2nd floor. Once they got out of the elevator, they used their card key to enter the spa. He and Andersen entered the men's locker room and placed their clothes into lockers and retained the laundry bag. Ragnhild entered the women's locker room, put her clothes inside a locker, and locked it.

Ericksen walked into the sauna carrying a plastic water bottle, a laundry bag filled with a small towel, and a CIA cyanide poison dart gun. A bodyguard sat next to Ryzhkov.

When Ragnhild opened the door to the sauna, the five-foot-five-inch blonde, blue-eyed thirty-five year old Norwegian beauty with a curvy nude body was on full display as she entered. Ryzhkov and the Russian foreign intelligence officer's eyes focused on her.

After a few minutes, she got up and turned to the Russians. In English, she said "I'll be back in a minute."

The forty-year old Russian bodyguard glanced at Ryzhkov and said in Russian "I think I'll talk to the lady. I'll be right back." The six-foot muscular Russian got up and left the sauna.

Ericksen recognized the perfect opportunity for action. He stood up, gently opened the laundry bag, placed his hand on the CIA dart gun without taking it out, and approached Ryzhkov.

Ericksen swiftly opened the laundry bag, pulled out the dart gun, looked directly at Ryzhkov, aimed it straight at Ryzhkov's heart, and said "Evgeny, Dimitri, and Viktor Sorokin have met their fate!" Ryzhkov's face turned shades of gray.

"Ericksen!" a surprised and frightened Ryzhkov yelled.

"Yes, you rotten bastard! You're going to die!" In two seconds, he squeezed the trigger to the dart gun, ejecting the frozen cyanide dart into the oligarch. Ryzhkov was in shock, grabbing his chest, and fell to the floor of the sauna. In thirty seconds, he was dead.

While Ericksen killed Ryzhkov, the scene near the lady's locker room was in play. Andersen left the men's locker room and walked toward Ragnhild, who was ten feet from the lady's locker room and flirting with the Russian. He removed the CIA cyanide poison dart gun from the laundry bag, squeezed the trigger, and the poison ejected into the back of the Russian spy's neck. The man fell to the ground dead.

Ericksen lifted Ryzhkov and placed him in a seated position leaning his body against the sauna's paneled wall. He surmised that anyone entering the sauna would probably contact the manager, fearing the man had died of a heart attack or stroke. That was the beauty of the cyanide poison dart.

Ericksen opened the sauna door and saw Andersen carrying the dead Russian security man into the sauna. He joined him and helped place the Russian on the upper row and lying down on the wooden bench next to Ryzhkov's body.

Just then, an elderly man and woman in their seventies and entered the sauna. Both Ericksen and Andersen smiled and left a few minutes later.

They went to their respective lockers, changed clothes, and walked to the elevator. Ragnhild and her husband went back to their room, and Ericksen took the stairs and departed from the hotel.

He called a number in Berlin and connected to a cyberhacking organization. Upon receiving his cell phone alert, both the NSA and unit 8200 re-activated the video cameras on the fifth floor, in the elevator, and in the spa area. Thirty minutes later, he opened the door to the vacation rental chalet in Saanen.

The Andersens' checked out of Chateau Rosenberg and met Ericksen at the chalet in Saanen. They were joined by Roubini and the female assassin.

One hour later, they were all on the road in two rental vehicles headed for Frankfurt.

The following day the Andersens flew to Oslo, Roubini and his lady operative flew to Tel Aviv, and Ericksen flew to Copenhagen.

Ericksen spent two nights with his aunt, uncle and cousins in Horsholm, Denmark, before departing back to the Bay Area.

ST. PETERSBURG, RUSSIA

On July 16, 2012, the Swiss government arranged to ship Alexander Ryzhkov's body to St. Petersburg, Russia. The medical examiner and the forensic team discovered the cyanide poison that caused /his death. The doctors sent a report to the president's office. President Gorshkov read the information and decided to fly to St. Petersburg for his friend's funeral.

The funeral took place on July 18, 2012. General Alexander Leonidovich Ryzhkov was buried in Tikhvin Cemetery in the center of Saint Petersburg. Ryzhkov's wife and adult children were in attendance and relatives, friends, and President Gorshkov. Many of the friends who grew up with Ryzhkov in St. Petersburg were present when President Gorshkov spoke in Russian at the gravesite: "Dear friends, today we are mourning a true Russian patriot, a great Russian general who served his country with integrity, courage, and dedication. Alexander Leonidovich Ryzhkov." His voice trembling, "Sasha was my best friend, and he will truly be missed."

Chapter Twenty-Six

GOTLAND ISLAND, SWEDEN

On August 22, Otto Schroeder arrived on his Italian yacht *Renate* and moored his thirty-six-meter boat at the Herrvik marina on Gotland Island. His valet picked him up and drove him back to his summer home which sat on a bluff near the village of Ljugarn, overlooking the harbor and the Baltic Sea. Schroeder became the CEO of the company following his father's death. He began preparation for the arrival of the Russian agents who planned to stay at his summer home the following week.

Mark Ericksen and Jeb Templeton arrived in Copenhagen on Thursday, August 30, from Chicago and were met by Thomas Andersen, the managing director of *Amundsen Security Group*, and Henning, his Danish general manager. Everyone got into Henning's van and drove to Ystad, Sweden. They pulled up to the Strindberg Inn, a resort hotel overlooking the harbor, and where Gunnar, *Amundsen Security Group's* Swedish general director, joined them. After getting situated, they made dinner reservations at an upscale restaurant in Ystad. Their dinner at the Villa Strandvagen of delicious Swedish meatballs, mashed potatoes, lingonberry sauce, and dessert, along with Aquavit and Tuborg beers.

On next day the men drove to Kaseberga, a fishing village near

Ystad. They got out of the Honda Odyssey van and began walking up a bluff overlooking the sea. Sitting on a ridge were large upright stones dating back over one thousand years. This site was known as Ales Stenar. Fifty-nine upright stones weighed at least one thousand pounds each. The story goes it was a Viking burial site. Another story says it is dedicated to the people who lost their lives at sea.

Breathing in the sea air, Templeton smiled and said, "the serenity of this place warms my soul." Ericksen looked at Templeton and the other men. He removed a California cabernet, five glasses, opened the wine bottle, and gently poured the red wine into each of the men's glasses. He raised his glass of wine and smiled. "Let us celebrate the joy that brings us together. The peace and our future destiny. Skoal."

"Andersen lifted his glass and spoke in English, "Let's toast to the *Andersen Security Group* and *Cyberburst Biometrics*. Skoal."

Turgenev and his team arrived on Gotland Island on August 28 and August 29. They were all staying at Schroeder's summer home on the east side of the Island. They immediately began reconnaissance and traveled the many roads that led to the airport from the conference center in Klintehamn. They also studied the roads leading back to the east side of the Island.

The *Cyberburst Biometrics* European distributors conference ran from September 5-7 in the Persson Resort. Distributors from Scandinavian countries, United Kingdom, France, Germany, The Netherlands, Portugal, Spain, Switzerland, Austria, Italy, and Greece, were represented. When the distributors arrived at the Persson Resort in Klintehamn, everything was planned: the schedule, the sales meetings, the strategies, new products, programs, incentives, etc.

On September 7, Ericksen and Templeton hired the Persson Resort driver to drive them to the airport outside of Visby. Their flight to Stockholm departs at 16:35. They left the resort at 13:45. The temperature was sixty degrees fahrenheit and sunny.

On highway 140 toward Tofta, about ten kilometers north of Klintehamn, a truck was blocking the road. Several cars were at a standstill. All of the truck's tires were shot out. Ericksen's driver slowed down, and immediately one van approached from the left side of their vehicle, and the other van bumped into their rear bumper. Suddenly, four men dressed in green fatigues and wearing masks jumped out of the vans. Ericksen suddenly glanced toward the driver, who was shot in the head by a very tall and muscular man. Then he turned toward Templeton as the same tall man raised his Sig-Sauer P- 226 handgun and fired three shots into Templeton's head. Blood sprayed everywhere. At that moment, one of the attackers fired a tranquilizer into Ericksen's shoulder through the open window of the vehicle. Then, pulled Ericksen out of the car, opened the van door, and threw him in. Everyone jumped back into their vans, drove a few kilometers south, and made a left turn at Bjars. They continued to drive east toward Roma and made a right turn onto highway 143, traveling southeast.

At this point, they had traveled about twenty-five kilometers. They drove another thirteen kilometers reaching the town of Suderbys and turned down a dirt road for about two kilometers until they reached a grassy area. Everyone got out of the vans and opened the doors of a new Toyota van. They carried the unconscious Ericksen to the awaiting van and placed him on the floor. Kirill got into Schroeder's Volvo rental.

"It doesn't look like anyone is following us," said Turgenev in Russian. A Russian looked up and raised his right thumb. They hurriedly drove back to Highway 143 and turned left, going south for twenty-three kilometers, turned left at Ljugarn for another two kilometers, and finally arrived at Schroeder's two-acre summer home. The van and the Volvo parked inside the two-car garage on the property. Two men carried Ericksen inside the house, tied him up, and placed him in a separate bedroom.

During the past sixty minutes, the Swedish police were called to the scene and began asking questions, followed by an ambulance, to retrieve the two dead men. One of the officers noticed the name on the van. They contacted Persson's resort and found out a conference just concluded. The two individuals transported to the Visby airport were two Americans, Jeb Templeton and Mark Ericksen. The Swedish National Police in Stockholm received the call about the abduction of the American, Mark Ericksen.

Within thirty minutes, the Swedish National Police contacted the American Embassy and the Swedish Security Service because it appeared to be an act of terrorism. A senior executive of the Sakerhet-spolisen, (SAPO), called the American Embassy's CIA station chief, informing him of the situation. An hour later, the CIA director at Langley, Virginia, contacted the Office of Director of National Intelligence, NSA, and Defense Secretary Sullivan.

The telephone rang at Sullivan's residence. On the fourth ring, he picked it up.

"Sorry, Secretary Sullivan, Mark Ericksen was abducted after leaving his distributor conference on Gotland Island. The attackers killed his general manager, Jeb Templeton."

"I'll be on my way to the ODNI right now," Sullivan said.

Andersen heard about the abduction an hour later. Gunnar contacted his old boss at SAPO and gave vital background information about the conference and the Americans. The Swedish Intelligence Agency, the NSA, and British Intelligence began cyber monitoring between Russian Intelligence sources.

An hour later when Sullivan arrived at the ODNI's headquarters in McClean, Virginia. He immediately talked with the Defense Intelligence Agency, NSA, and the US Special Forces Command. Everyone started monitoring the situation. Sullivan contacted the Swedish defense minister and requested them to send helicopters and drones to see if they could spot the attackers' vehicles. The American defense department immediately activated the satellite tracking system to fly over the east side of Gotland Island.

Two hours later, a commander of the National Reconnaissance Office picked up a signal pulsing from Ericksen's implanted RFID tracking device from an area near Tofta, on Gotland Island. A few hours later, a pulse-sensing signal emanated from an area near Ljugard.

On Saturday, September 8, the Swedish National Police had Templeton's body flown to an airstrip outside of Copenhagen. Three hours later, an American government aircraft flew Templeton's body back to Portland, Oregon, where his wife and close friends were awaiting his body to be picked up and sent to a mortuary.

Turgenev pulled out his encrypted satellite phone, walked out to the lawn, and called the Russian military intelligence operations command center (GRU) in Moscow.

"Yes, Bear02. We've been waiting for your call."

"We have just arrived. The plan is to depart from the marina tomorrow evening around 2200 hours. When are you leaving St. Petersburg?" said Turgenev.

"The frigate *Lev Tolstoy*, a Grigorovich class, will depart today and meet you at the following coordinates 58.4219. and 020.5994, roughly eighty kilometers northwest of Undva, Saaremaa, Estonia, around 0530 hours on Monday, September 10."

"Thanks." Said Turgenev.

Turgenev and one of his men untied Ericksen and gave him some fresh air on the property. President Gorshkov told him to treat Ericksen with respect and care. They were out for an hour, and then he brought Ericksen back inside and seated him for dinner. After dinner, he was tied up again and placed in a separate bedroom under guard.

NSA and GCHQ just accessed and retrieved the GRU communications and informed the Director of National Intelligence in McLean, Virginia. All communications immediately went out to the Secretary of Defense Sullivan, CIA director, Joint Special Operations Command, other Intelligence agencies and departments, and the ministries of defense of Norway, Denmark, and Sweden.

A new flash came in from the National Reconnaissance Office identifying Ericksen's sensing device again near the town of Ljugard. "It is apparent Russian intelligence operatives abducted Ericksen and will be leaving shortly from one of the marinas in the area," said Sullivan.

"We need to identify the Russians' ship that's planning to rendevous with the frigate *Lev Tolstoy* at coordinates 58.4219 and 020.5994 on Monday, September 10 at 0530 hours," said the National Intelligence Director.

The Secretary of the Navy spoke up, "Currently, the Danish Royal Navy's *Absalon* frigate class, the Swedish Royal Navy's *Goteborg* corvette class vessel, the Norwegian Royal Navy's *Fridtjof Nansen* class frigate, and the American Arleigh Burke-class guided-missile destroyer *USS Banbridge* are taking part of a training exercise thirty miles north of Gotland Island.

Furthermore, Sullivan learned that SEAL Team-3 was part of a training exercise with the Royal Danish Navy's Frogman Corps in Rodvig, Denmark. Sullivan placed a conference call to the Secretary of the Navy and the United States Special Operations Commander.

"Mobilize SEAL Team-3 at Rodvig and helo them to the *USS Banbridge* immediately!"

"Yes, sir!"

On Sunday, September 9, at 2100 hours, Otto Schroeder, Turgenev, and three Russian Intelligence operatives shoved a tranquilized Ericksen into the van and drove north to the Herrvik marina, where the *Renate* was docked. They carried him on board the mega yacht. Turgenev sent a radio communique to the Russian frigate *Lev Tolstoy* of the Grigorovich class. "We will be departing at 2200 hours on the *Renate*. We will head northeast at 18 knots and look forward to meeting up with you."

The Russian frigate commander, a Captain, first rank, replied, "Confirming, the rendezvous point will be eighty kilometers due northwest of Estonia's island Saaremaa. We departed from St. Petersburg five hours ago and should meet your *Renate* between 0530 to 0600 hours Swedish time."

At 2200 hours, the yacht *Renate* sailed out of the marina and headed due northeast toward Estonia. Ericksen had his hands tied behind his back and sat on a chair while Turgenev sized him up. "Do you have any idea why you were abducted, Mr. Ericksen?"

"No. You tell me?"

"Our President wants to meet you personally. Once we arrive in St. Petersburg, you'll be transported to a jet and flown to Moscow to meet President Gorshkov. You must be an important man to have our President interested in meeting you," said Turgenev.

"You were the asshole who shot and killed my good friend Jeb. You also shot and killed a Swedish civilian. You are the scum of the earth!"

Turgenev walked over to Ericksen and slapped his face so hard Ericksen and the chair fell over.

"Who do you think you are talking to, Mr. Ericksen?"

"I'm Igor Turgenev, the deputy director of the FSB."

"Excuse me. Now, why don't you go fuck yourself!"

Turgenev's face turned red with anger, and he walked up and smashed Ericksen with a right cross, landing on his cheek and knocking him down. Ericksen stayed on the floor for a while until Kirill picked him up along with the chair.

At 2300 hours, Sunday, September 9, Swedish time, eight SEAL Team-3 operators were being flown by the Royal Danish Navy in a Sikorsky 60H Seahawk helicopter. NSA sent a communications brief to all intelligence agencies and departments: "An hour ago we picked up another signal pulsing from Ericksen's RFID tracking device around the Herrvik marina. There was only one boat that left the marina. We identified it as the *Renate*, a mega yacht around 35 or 36 meters in length."

At 0145 hours, Monday, September 10, the eight SEAL Team-3 operators rappelled from the Seahawk helicopter to the *USS Banbridge*. They were now about fifty miles from the *Renate* heading due East toward Estonia.

At 0400 hours, two rigid inflatable boats, better known as Zodiacs, entered the waters manned by a coxswain controlling the outboard engine's tiller arm, while four Navy SEAL operators got into each boat and were fully armed. The Zodiacs were eight kilometers from the *Renate*.

At 0430, one Zodiac pulled alongside the port side, and the other perfectly matched the time on the starboard side. They both threw a hook with an attached ladder to the deck and climbed aboard. One of the SEAL operators spotted a crew member standing guard. He aimed and fired two shots from his Heckler and Koch sub-machine gun, which had a suppressor on it. The guard fell dead on the deck, blood flowing from his wounds to the head and back. The SEAL team operators combed the lower and main decks, opening cabin doors, shocking two Russian FSB operatives, who immediately tried to grab their Makarov handguns. They were both shot dead. Next, two SEALs opened up a cabin occupied with two crewmen. One of the SEALs held his finger to his lips and said, "Get on the floor." The other SEAL operator flex cuffed their hands behind them and lifted them on the bed. One of the SEALs stood guard.

In the next cabin were more crewmen, and the same scene took place. Two SEALs burst onto the bridge and took charge of the captain and his two officers. Two SEALS burst onto the cabin on the main deck where Ericksen was being held.

Kirill turned around, attempted to fire his gun and was shot dead by a SEAL. The other SEAL untied Ericksen, and gave him his Sig-Sauer handgun.

"Thank you," said Ericksen. He put his slacks, shirt, socks, and brown oxford shoes on.

They walked toward the captain's cabin and burst into the large room. Turgenev woke up and was surprised to see Ericksen and a special forces operator with him. Ericksen handed the gun to the SEAL.

"If I don't come out, kill him!"

"Affirmative," the SEAL replied. Ericksen closed the cabin door.

"You must be proud of yourself for hitting someone tied to a chair. I have to admit, you look like a very strong and tough son-of-a-bitch. Let's go man-to-man Igor."

Ericksen's face was full of anger. "To the death!"

"I am going to kill you with my bare hands," chuckled Turgenev.

The Russian suddenly charged Ericksen, and he swiftly moved to his left and tripped Turgenev, who fell to the floor and quickly bounced back up. Turgenev raced toward Ericksen, landing a right to Ericksen's forehead, as he exchanged blows with the Russian. Blood started flowing from Ericksen's forehead. Turgenev charged him, but Ericksen swiftly moved to his right, and kicked the Russian's knee, and threw a right to his kidneys. Turgenev stood for a moment and then charged at Ericksen again, landing a left to his jaw, and a right to

Ericksen's chest, sending him back against a bookcase. Ericksen regained his balance, as Turgenev grabbed a steel rod and attempted to hit his head, but the former Navy SEAL operator moved to his left, kicked the Russian's knee, and threw a mighty right hand cutting Turgenev's mouth, another kick to the Russian's groin, followed by a left to his nose, and a karate chop to his neck. Suddenly, Ericksen tackled him to the ground, pummeling his face several times. Turgenev's broken nose bled freely all over his face and body. He reached for his knife with his right hand, which was on the floor beneath the bed. Ericksen spotted the eight-inch sharp-bladed knife, and grabbed Turgenev's hand holding the knife as they struggled for control. He kneed the Russian's groin a couple of times, elbowed his jaw, and immediately managed to take the knife from Turgenev. He gripped the knife in his right hand and thrust the blade into Turgenev's neck. Blood squirted out all over the place. Ericksen pulled the knife from his neck and plunged it into Turgenev's heart, killing him. He stood up over the dead Russian's body.

The Russian frigate arrived at 0530 hours and spotted the American destroyer following the *Renate* back toward Sweden. The commander immediately called President Gorshkov with the news.

"The *USS Banbridge* has sabotaged our operations."

"Captain, you just lost your command!" said Gorshkov.

At 1700 hours, a Swedish Royal Navy ship approached and ten crewmen boarded the *Renate* forty kilometers east of Stockholm. Four members of the Swedish intelligence service (SAPO) and five Swedish Police Authority members were with them. They arrested Otto Schroeder and the German crew members. A Swedish Royal Navy Coast Guard boat picked up the eight SEAL Team-3 operators, Ericksen and delivered them back to the *USS Banbridge*. Ericksen told the Swedish authorities it was Igor Turgenev, deputy director of the FSB and three of his operatives who killed the Swedish driver and Jeb Templeton.

Ericksen and the eight SEAL Team-3 operators arrived in Copenhagen via a US Air Force helicopter at 2100 hours. On Tuesday, September 11, Ericksen boarded Secretary of Defense Sullivan's Gulfstream G550 jet for the flight back to Portland, Oregon. On the flight back, Ericksen thought about losing his good friend and his best man at his wedding. He remembered his last JSOC mission in Afghanistan in April 2002. Major Templeton was his squadron commander of the Bravo Team on a high-value targets mission in a mountainous region near Khost, Afghanistan. In 2006, it was Templeton's recommendation that helped him get the job at *EyeD4 Systems*. He was saddened about the tragic death, the murder of his good friend. He needed to be there to console Templeton's wife and children.

The Swedish Foreign Ministry contacted the Russian Ambassador to inform him to retrieve the four dead Russian intelligence operatives who murdered a Swedish citizen and an American businessman. President Gorshkov received the news an hour later and ordered the Russian embassy to retrieve their bodies and have them flown back to Moscow.

Chapter Twenty-Seven

PALO ALTO

On Tuesday, November 13, Logan Mitchell, COO of *Cyberburst Communications,* announced his resignation due to ill health. The Santa Clara County Courthouse schedule was overloaded, and Mitchell appearing this year was not likely to happen. He posted a bail of $1 million, relinquished his passport to the court because the court deemed him a flight risk. Then the court placed an electronic GPS ankle bracelet around his right ankle.

On Friday, November 30, 2012, Kastrup, with the board of director's approval, appointed Mark Ericksen to the position of executive vice-president and chief operating officer of the company. His new salary was $1million per year and a massive increase in shares of stock. The news of this event went viral on social media, the *Wall Street Journal, Forbes, Fortune magazine, New York Times, Barron's, Reuters, Bloomberg Businessweek, London Financial Times, the BBC News, Los Angeles Times* and local newspapers in Silicon Valley, San Jose, and San Francisco.

THE G8 SUMMIT, NORTHERN IRELAND

The G8 leaders were meeting on June 17-18, 2013 in Lough Erne on the shore in County Fermanagh, Northern Ireland. The American President Porterfield agreed to meet Russian President Mikhail Gorshkov an hour before the G8 Summit was scheduled to start in a resort conference room.

Porterfield was accompanied by Secretary of Defense Bill Sullivan, and Sullivan's chief-of-staff. Gorshkov was joined by his foreign minister and translator.

Gorshkov was a master in the art of persuasive and manipulative communications. The American delegation was suspicious of anything the Russian president proposed. After all, Gorshkov had accelerated his power over the military, the intelligence service, politicians, oligarchs, and organized crime networks.

The last thing he wanted to do was acknowledge his approval of assassinations of members of the CIA's *Operations Avenging Eagles*. Nor did he want to mention the men who had died at the hands of Ericksen and his colleagues.

They entered the resort conference center and walked to the executive boardroom for their meeting. Everyone shook hands and sat down around a large u-shaped oak conference table. Porterfield looked straight at him and said, "President Gorshkov, we come here in peace and want to maintain dialogue between our two great countries. However, you must immediately stop any future assassinations against our citizens and stop any plans to invade any former Soviet Union countries. Otherwise, we will have no choice but to implement severe sanctions against your country."

Gorshkov's face turned red. The muscular head of Russia looked like a man you never wanted to cross. He looked at the American president, then turned and starred at Secretary of Defense Sullivan.

"I don't know what you're talking about. Look, I don't want any more trouble, but you have to realize the destruction of the Soviet Union by the West had terrible consequences for the future of the Russian Federation."

President Porterfield nodded and replied, "I understand what you've been experiencing for the past twenty-two years. However, we have a chance to develop better relations and improve our peoples lives. Give us that chance."

Gorshkov nodded and looked at Porterfield and Sullivan. "Let's try to understand each other and make an effort to work together to solve our differences."

"President Gorshkov, You and your Kremlin cronies supported a Saudi terrorist mastermind who planned on attacking two American cities with nuclear suitcase bombs. Why would you condone this horrific act?" asked President Porterfield.

"I don't know anything about this man or that operation."

"You may wish to deny having any knowledge of the planned operation but let me inform you, if that operation had been successful many Americans would have died. Those two cities would have incurred massive destruction," said President Porterfield.

Gorshkov knew that the CIA's *Operation Avenging Eagles* mission had derailed his Middle East plans. He raised his voice. "As long as you have influence around our borders, we will have problems with your country."

They continued their discussions over the next ten minutes. Gorshkov looked directly at Sullivan.

"We've had encouraging dialogue and many constructive conversations in 1996 and 1997 at diplomatic parties in Moscow, and after the G8 meeting of July 15-17, 2006 in St. Petersburg. You were then the CIA director under President Ridgeway, and I invited you to play against me in a couple of handball matches the next day at my favorite club's handball courts in St. Petersburg," said Gorshkov.

"I remember those happy occasions. Those are fond memories. However, today you have a chance of giving your people a taste of democracy, or you can stay the course as a dictator and suffer the consequences. It is really up to you, President Gorshkov."

"The people voted me into office. We're trying to improve their quality of life and increase employment opportunities."

Gorshkov stopped his train of thought and smiled. "Some people have mentioned to me there is talk you might be running for president in 2016. Is that true?"

"No." Sullivan said in Russian, "It's is a rumor. If it became a reality, I wouldn't be surprised to find you meddling in our elections like you do in Europe."

"You can't believe everything you hear," said Gorshkov.

"Assuming for a moment it was true, as a registered independent, I would have to decide on running as a Democrat or as a Republican. I understand the former secretary of state is next in line to run as a Democrat in 2016. I know there will probably be a broad lineup of governors and senators running in the race. Can you believe there is even a wealthy hotel developer who used to be a television reality star who plans to run as a Republican. If I run for president in 2016 as a Republican and won, I would nominate Mark Ericksen to become the secretary of defense. I'm sure that would make your day!"

"Your sense of humor isn't always appreciated," replied Gorshkov. "Which brings me to the last topic of discussion," Sullivan said. He turned to his chief-of-staff. "Ask Ericksen to enter."

Fifteen seconds later, the executive vice-president and COO of *Cyberburst Communications* entered the room with confidence.

President Gorshkov's eyes became focused on Ericksen as his face tightened and he became motionless. He stood up, and his face and body looked like a stone sculpture. Sullivan stared intensely at Gorshkov.

"Let me introduce you to Mark Ericksen."

Ericksen reached his right hand out to shake President Gorshkov's hand.

"I met Igor Turgenev last year while cruising on the yacht named *Renate*. Turgenev told me you were personally looking forward to meeting me. Well, I must say it is a pleasure to meet you President Gorshkov," said Ericksen with a smile.

Gorshkov had the look of anger as he stopped his scrowl and struggled to smile. "Yes, Mr. Ericksen."

President Porterfield, Secretary Sullivan, the Russian foreign minister, and Ericksen stared at each other for a moment. Then

Sullivan smiled as Gorshkov smiled grimly. They shook hands and walked away without saying another word.

One month later, Secretary of Defense Sullivan announced his retirement from government service, effectively departing on August 15th.

IRVINE, CALIFORNIA

The board of directors of *G5 Defense Systems*, a major aerospace and defense corporation with headquarters in Irvine, California, has appointed William Sullivan, the former secretary of defense, to the position of CEO and president of the corporation. Its most recent annual revenues reached $150 billion. The media reported that Mr. Sullivan would start on October 1, 2013.

PALO ALTO

On October 15, the board of directors of *Cyberburst Communications* announced that Poul Kastrup was retiring from the company and maintaining the board of directors' chairmanship. He announced the appointment of Mark Ericksen to be the president and CEO of the company, effective November 1, 2013.

Epilogue

WILLIAM SULLIVAN

On a rainy day in July 2015, Bill Sullivan and his wife sat on lounge chairs on their patio in Laguna Beach, California overlooking the Pacific Ocean. They were drinking margaritas and eating burritos. As President/CEO of *G5 Defense Systems*, he was proud of the accolades the company received as it became one of the defense and aerospace industries' stars performers these past two years. Sullivan was gaining prominence in the media because of his company's successful performance and diverse acquisitions. Many government officials from the Republican Party, corporate CEOs, television network anchors, and current party officials encouraged him to run in the upcoming presidential election of 2016.

Sullivan discussed with his family the pros and cons. On Saturday, August 22, 2015, Sullivan announced his candidacy for president. Republican candidates running in this race were: former governors, current senators, two businessmen, and a wealthy former reality tv star and current Florida hotel developer.

By the end of April 2016, the race narrowed between the Florida hotel developer and Sullivan. Many Republican delegates recognized

Sullivan had an excellent government background in foreign affairs, intelligence, and defense. He was also a military veteran.

The wealthy hotel developer had no government experience, and his business empire suffered many bankruptcies. By mid-May, 2016, Sullivan developed a lead over his opponent.

MARK ERICKSEN

One sunny day in May 2016, Mark Ericksen, his wife Kate, their four-year-old daughter Anne, two-year-old son Jeb, and their dog Ava strolled along Dunes Beach in Half Moon Bay, California. Anne and Jeb enjoyed getting their feet wet in the waves and running out back. These precious family moments have meant a lot to Mark and Kate. His company Cyberburst Communications had revenues that reached thirty billion. As President/CEO of the company, the forty-six-year-old executive couldn't be happier, running an exciting Silicon Valley company and having a wonderful family. His wife Kate worked as a wealth management executive for a Swiss bank. They hired a nanny three years ago and enjoyed living in Menlo Park.

WASHINGTON D.C.

On May 23, 2016, Bill Sullivan called Ericksen and asked if he could meet him on June 1 at the Ritz-Carleton for dinner. On Memorial Day, Sullivan visited his son's grave at Arlington National Cemetery. Captain Ryan Sullivan, US Marines, was born December 20, 1977, and died August 5, 2005. Sullivan knelt beside the gravestone and placed a bouquet of red roses against it. His son was killed in Anbar Province, Iraq.

Later that day, Mark Ericksen visited the grave at Arlington National Cemetery of his Navy SEAL Team-Six buddy, petty officer first class, Vincent Goldman. Goldman's gravestone had a Jewish Star of David on top. He was born March 25, 1973, and died on April 18, 2002, on a tier-1 JSOC mission near Khost, Afghanistan. He died in Ericksen's arms.

Sullivan met with Ericksen at the Ritz-Carlton Hotel in George-town. He asked Ericksen if he would be his secretary of defense should he win the presidential election. Ericksen said he'd be honored.

On July 19, 2016 at the Republican National Convention, Sullivan received 1,500 states' delegate votes, exceeding the 1,237 needed to win. He officially became the nominee for president and the former lady Republican secretary of state from 2005-2009, became the nominee for vice-president.

PRESIDENT MIKHAIL GORSHKOV

President Mikhail Gorshkov didn't want the former Democratic secretary of state to win and approved of a disinformation campaign circulated throughout social media about her. Gorshkov wanted the Florida hotel developer to win because he believed he would spread enough lies, confusion, and conspiracies to undermine U.S. Democracy and divide the American people.

When election results were announced that his old acquaintance William Sullivan won the presidency, he knew the next four years would be stressful. Gorshkov also knew the risks involved, should he attempt to invade and occupy Ukraine and the Baltic States. When the Soviet Union was dismantled, those countries sought their independence. Gorshkov's dream was to take them back and place them under the Russian Federation.

PRESIDENT-ELECT WILLIAM SULLIVAN

On November 8, 2016, Sullivan beat the former Democratic secretary of state and became the Republican president-elect. His running mate was the former Republican secretary of state during 2005-2009. President Gorshkov called Sullivan and congratulated him on his victory.

On January 20, 2017, President William "Bill" Sullivan was sworn in as the 45th president of the United States. Three weeks later, Mark Ericksen received enough Senate votes to be confirmed as the next secretary of defense of the United States.

THE WHITE HOUSE SITUATION ROOM

On June 20, 2017, satellite pictures from the National Reconnaissance Office (NRO) confirmed that about 20,000 Russian soldiers moved from Ostrov, Russia, and are currently five miles from the Latvian border. Secretary of Defense Ericksen informed Sullivan, the Intelligence Community, and the Secretary of State. Sullivan concluded a meeting in the Situation Room and ordered Ericksen to take action.

Fifteen minutes later, Ericksen ordered the United States Special Operations Command to deploy 1,000 troops from Germany to Latvia. The Secretary-General of NATO and the U.S. Supreme Allied Commander in Europe was advised by President Sullivan to commence plans for missiles and tanks to be deployed if necessary.

On Wednesday, June 21, at 12:05 am, President Sullivan called Russian President Gorshkov (9:05 am Moscow time) from the Situation Room. He told him to cease operations immediately unless he wants a military confrontation at the Latvian border.

"President Sullivan, as I told you a minute ago, this is just a military training exercise," Gorshkov said.

"President Gorshkov, please don't test the American and NATO determination to defend Latvian sovereignty!"

"President Sullivan, the training exercise will be over in seven hours."

"Thank you and goodbye," said Sullivan.

Their telephone call ended. An understanding between the two superpower leaders had been reached, and the situation was resolved for now.

Afterword

Dear Reader,

I hope you enjoyed reading my novel, "The Ryzhkov Vendetta." If you would like to review and rate my book on Amazon.com, please go to the Amazon.com website. Key-in "The Ryzhkov Vendetta."

When you reach the page, please scroll down to the section [write a customer review]. Letting me know what you think of my book is very much appreciated.

Thank you,

Barry L. Becker

Acknowledgments

A special thanks to my editor, Michael J. Totten. *The Ryzhkov Vendetta* benefited significantly from his professional editing, keen observation of the major plots, and input based on his foreign correspondent experience as a journalist in the Middle East.

A special thanks to my wife, who provided me additional editing, unwavering love, and support.

About the Author

The author riding in a London Eye capsule over the River Thames
with a view of the British House of Parliament building in the
background.

Barry L. Becker retired in 2013 after spending twenty years as a sole proprietor for an independent manufacturers' representative company in Oregon. Also, he has provided marketing consulting services for corporations in the biometrics technology industry.

Mr. Becker previously served as vice-president of international sales and marketing from 1984 to 1991 for *Eyedentify,* an Oregon company specializing in eye-retinal scanning technology for positive ID in sensitive facilities.

In 1987, he wrote an article entitled *"Eyedentify Counters Security Threat,"* which appeared in the Journal of Defense and Diplomacy.

The Ericksen Connection is A Mark Ericksen Thriller Book 1.

The Ryzhkov Vendetta is A Mark Ericksen Thriller Book 2.